Mooi

EM Harding

ISBN: 9781693007729

First Edition

This book was a marathon that I frequently tried to sprint, so I dedicate it to those who made me stop, have a drink and eat a biscuit.

*The Moon fell into the Ocean and the Waves
wept. Their tears swept the lands clean and left
the World feeling painfully empty. And so, to fill
the aching void, the World gave birth to us, the
people of Infinity. The World smiled and danced
around the Stars with joy.*

That's the story we tell children when they ask how
Infinity came to be. It's the fairy tale we were told to
tell. A bedtime story for tiny tots. If children ask why
the Moon fell, their parents shuffle awkwardly and say
it was a silly Moon, or a sleepy Moon. They don't tell
them the truth.

The truth would give them nightmares.

Hell, I'm thirty-seven and it still gives me
nightmares.

Every time I close my eyes, I find myself walking
toward my cabin door. There's an angry red light
coming through the windows and the metal walls are
humming with energy. As I touch the latch, I feel
every hair stand upright. My skin tingles.

I push the door open and step out onto the deck. I
look at the Moon. It's glowing. I've never seen it glow

before. Part of me wants to run back to my computer to check the readings, but something stronger is pulling me away from the old cargo ship I call home and down onto the pontoon.

Before I know it, I'm running along the floating jetty, out into the middle of the ocean. The waters are completely still. No waves. Not even a ripple from my weight skittering along the surface. I pause and look down. No face looks back at me. I feel my nose wrinkle and my brow furrow, but I don't see it. So I continue running. And running.

The Moon sits two miles off the southern coast of Infinity's single mass continent. The original scientists that held our moon-sitting posts positioned most of the bases far enough away that they would have time to send a warning, should the Moon cause another unnatural disaster. Hector resides in the shipping container five miles from the shore, and Belle lives ten miles inland, in an old caravan. The cargo ship, however, positioned itself right on the beach. I think we'd all prefer it to be further away from the Moon, but it was too useful not to convert for moon-sitting.

As I run, I think of my fellow moon-sitters. I wonder if they're watching, if they see me sprinting. They must think I'm mad. My dark skin and scutes flake away, revealing ice-white flesh and new, pearly horn. I worry that the light from the Moon is burning me away, but it doesn't hurt.

Then comes the moment where I'm standing at the foot of the Moon. I've never been there in real life. Council law dictates that we must stay away from the

Moon unless given special permission. Moon-sitters can only break this law in an emergency, or else face imprisonment. See, the enormous spherical structure isn't actually a moon. Not really. We don't know what it is, just that it didn't so much fall as land with a big enough bump to send tsunamis and earthquakes skittering across our planet's surface.

In my dreams, the jetty ends two feet from the Moon's smooth, clean face. I have to hold my hand over my eyes and squint to look at it through the scarlet light. Now I'm close, I feel the vibrations coming from the Moon in my bones. It makes me feel like the world is swimming and I throw up into the sea. I wipe my mouth and stand tall, trying to get my footing back. I breathe deeply – in through my nose, out through my mouth – and reach my hand out towards the Moon. I hover the scutes on my knuckles an inch from the surface. I can't feel any heat, so I touch it.

Noise explodes out of the Moon. It blasts me away and, as I slide arse-backwards along the pontoon, I see the waves rise high above me, like two enormous hands reaching out of the ocean. They slam down onto my chest, pulling me and the bridge under the water. I see the metal and plastic tear in two and wonder how I'm still alive. Then I blink myself awake.

Almost every morning since I moved here, I've woken

up covered in sweat, with the taste of salt water in my mouth. I stumble to the bathroom, check my reflection has returned, shower and swill my mouth out with root water. We Infinitians haven't quite gotten around to figuring out how to make dental cleaner again yet. It's been on the to-do list for a while; the public supply ran out when I was still a kid.

Body and mouth clean, I return to my living quarters and turn on my computer. Marcus – who was the ship's original tenant and my mentor – built the machine from parts found in Infinity's last remaining city. He built similar setups in the shipping container and caravan too, as well as setting up the wind turbines that power everything here. Infinity was fortunate enough to have a number of good minds, people who understood how things worked, survive the Moon's arrival, but things are still not quite the same.

This morning, when I turn on my computer, it brings up the usual readings: a consistent low-level vibration, standard temperature, no signs of life. The Moon is an angry black hole on my screen. I pull back my curtains and look at it through the window. Even half-submerged in the ocean, it's gigantic. The Moon looms over everything along the coast as far as the eye can see, with its summit five miles above sea level and its diameter a perfect ten miles wide. At certain times of year I get very little direct light.

Most people in City have only ever seen the Moon in pictures. They're lucky. In the early days, they ran a few small memorial trips for folks to pay their respects. Not many people were interested in going anywhere near the Moon, but Mum brought me when I was still young. Funnily enough, I think the nightmares started after that, but back then it was just me running in the dark. I'm fast, but I think I had to run so far that I never quite understood what I was running to, until I returned to start my moon-sitting apprenticeship with Marcus.

I sit down at my desk and send a message to Hector and Belle:

L: Good morning. Same old sphere. You?

I lean back in my chair. There are some phosphorescent stars on the ceiling that I rescued from my bedroom in the Marshlands. Marcus thought they were childish. I don't think those rules apply anymore; everyone needs a security blanket.

H: Same old sphere. Anyone got flour? I'm short on bread.
B: Same old sphere. Don't look at me. I've been living on ration packets for the last month.
L: We should try and grow crops here again.
B: And waste more seed? I don't think City would like that.
H: Well then, City needs to bring supplies faster.
L: Someone's hungry.
H: Hungry and constipated. The lack of fibre is killing me.

I laugh. There was a time when we didn't share such

information, but the three of us have been alone out here for seven years now. It's what we all signed up for. We arrived at the grand old age of twenty, trained with our mentors until thirty, and now we're on our own until the next batch of apprentices turn up at forty. It's not like we never get to go back to City, though. We take it in turns to visit. They send a solarflyer on four round trips a year to drop supplies and give one of us a short break. The rest of the time we sit here, relatively alone, each of us staring at a screen monitoring the outputs from our friend, the Moon.

> **L:** Party on the cargo ship this evening?
> **H:** Sure. Let's live dangerously. Shall I bring cards?
> **B:** Only if you don't cheat this time!
> **H:** Isabelle! For the last time, the game is called 'Menace' because you are supposed to menace each other, i.e. lie, cheat and steal points.
> **B:** All of which seems to come so naturally to you!

As they bicker, I find myself thinking there's no two people I'd rather be marooned at the edge of the continent with.

The first time I met Hector and Belle was on the deck of the cargo ship in the dark season. I'd been on the southern coast with Marcus for a week already, and was eager to meet my fellow trainees.

"Hello! Hello! How are you both? Did you have a good trip?" I sang as I bounced out onto the deck to greet them.

I realised almost immediately, however, that they were not so keen to meet me. Or, in fact, to be aboard the cargo ship. My bright smile and extended hand were met with withering glances.

"How can you possibly be so chipper?" Hector said glumly.

Belle – who had her arms wrapped around herself, bracing against the wind – didn't say anything. She was too busy scanning the rest of her environment, everything except the Moon behind her.

"You'll have to forgive Lucky," Marcus said, stumbling out of the cabin. "She's one of those rare nuts that loves her work." He was trying desperately to knot his hair into a bun on the back of his head. "Of course, I'm the other rare nut, which is why she ended up with me." Satisfied that his hair was firmly locked in place, Marcus extended his hand. "I'm Marcus. You must be Hector." They grabbed each other's forearms and shook twice, then Marcus turned. "And you must be Isabelle." Marcus extended his fingers like he was trying to coax a warren-hopper out of its den.

Gingerly, Belle reached out and shook his arm. "Y-yes."

Marcus clapped and Belle jumped. "Right! No point standing out here in the freezing cold. Elena and Titan won't be here for a while yet. Come on, I've got a hot pot of starspice brew inside."

We shuffled into the cabin and I pulled out the seats around Marcus' table. Marcus pottered about, spreading out cups and pouring the brew. The liquid made the air smell warm and comforting. I'd never had starspice before living with Marcus. It was practically impossible to get hold of, like any other spice on Infinity, but Marcus had his ways. Hector and Belle sniffed it suspiciously. I took a small sip and felt the peppered sweetness dance across my tongue. I grinned at the gloomy pair. "It's not poison."

"And if it were, then at least you wouldn't be at the edge of Infinity anymore." Marcus winked.

I scowled at him. "That's not funny."

Hector huffed out a short laugh. "It is." He took a mouthful of brew and swilled it around before swallowing. Then he let out a deep sigh. "Damn. Still here."

Belle took a gentle sip. Her eyes widened. "This is really good."

"One of the perks of living dangerously." Marcus rested his nose on the edge of his cup. "I'll miss this when I'm back in City. Still, that's a long way off yet. Tell me, where are you two from?"

Hector looked at Belle. She nodded for him to go first. "I'm from the Cracked Mountain village, just north of City."

"Ah, yes! I lived a touch further north with my orbital ... before the Moon, you understand. That explains your broad shoulders."

Hector grimaced. "Yeah, Dad used to make me work

in the quarry whenever I was home from school."

"Excellent. And you, Isabelle?"

"I'm from City," she said quietly. "My mother and father work security on the harvest halls."

"Ah." Marcus nodded. Clearly that explained something else to him, but he didn't say what. "It's a difficult job, that."

"They're both quite good at it. Mother won a commendation for taking down a flash-heist last year."

"Whoa," Hector muttered. "Flash-heists are only planned in the minutes before. How did she stop that?"

"Good instincts." Marcus grinned.

Belle smiled at the bottom of her cup.

"What about you, Lucky?" Hector asked.

"Oh, I'm one of the swamp people," I joked.

"You're from the Marshlands?" Belle looked at me curiously. I knew why. I don't exactly look like I'm from the Marshlands.

"That's where I grew up," I explain. "I don't exactly know where I was born. Or who my parents are. My last name's Marsh."

"I'm sorry," Belle murmured, going slightly pale.

I laughed. "Don't worry. I've long come to terms with being adopted."

At that moment, Elena threw open the cabin door and a gust of wind blew papers around the cabin. I scrambled up to get them.

"Elena, amicus! You do like to make an entrance. I'm sorry, Lucky. I should have used a paperweight." Marcus gestured for Elena to take a seat. She had to duck through the door. Behind her, the short, stout form of Titan tottered in the wind. "Titan, you too! Get in here," Marcus yelled.

Titan pulled himself in and slammed the door shut. "We're going to have to stay here until the storm blows over."

"It's hardly a storm," Elena grunted, stretching her legs out in front of her.

A rumble of thunder shook the metal cabin. Titan looked at Elena smugly. She rolled her eyes.

"Tut, tut, Elena. You know better than to tell the master of probability he's wrong," Marcus teased.

"One day I'll be right."

"It'll be a dark day in the light season," Titan whispered to Belle as he sat down.

Belle snorted into her drink, then whispered, "Sorry."

"Don't you get a lot of dark days in the light season here?" Hector asked. "What with that sitting out there, blocking all the sun?" He pointed out of the window at the Moon.

Elena grinned. "I like this one, Marcus. Is he mine?"

"Of course. Hector, Elena. Elena, Hector."

"That must make you my mentee." Titan poured Belle another cup of brew from the pot. "I'm Titan, but please, call me T. Titan has always seemed far too big a name."

"I'm Belle."

"Pleasure to meet you, Belle. So what brought you to the end of the continent?" T's voice was light, but his face was sympathetic, like he'd already predicted her answer.

"Oh, I, I chose to be here."

T nodded and placed a hand on her shoulder. "I had those parents too, don't worry."

Belle looked up at him and blinked in surprise. "How – "

"The longer you spend down here, the better you get at selecting the correct scenario."

Belle looked furtively between myself and Marcus, then leant over and whispered something in T's ear. He smiled. "Don't worry, Belle. I always thought Marcus was suspicious too, but having worked here for ten years I can assure you he's just a bit bonkers. This one here will be the same, I expect. Something in that red hair of theirs."

Belle sunk lower in her seat. T looked at myself and Marcus and tutted at himself. "I probably shouldn't have said that out loud." He turned his face and hid behind his cup of brew.

Marcus and I shared a glance. He'd told me that the new moon-sitters were character matched with their mentors, but I hadn't quite grasped how similar they'd be to Elena and T. We stared at each other, holding in our laughter.

"Will you two stop having a moment?" Elena smacked my thigh with her knee.

"Yeah, grinning like that is why we all think you're weird," Hector remarked.

Belle laughed quietly.

Marcus coughed and shook his head, then turned to the rest of the group. "Well, as you're staying with us weirdoes, how about some weird food? These two came with fresh supplies, so I can afford to make my surprise scramble."

T gave him a scathing look. "I'll cook."

"Oh?" Marcus looked innocent. "Do you think I'll give everyone food poisoning?"

"Absolutely," Elena snapped.

"Again," T grumbled, got up and began stumbling around Marcus' tiny kitchen.

By eight o'clock, Belle, Hector and I have eaten and our card game has turned into a drinking game. Turns out the other reason Hector is short on fibre is because he's been using his tuber ration to make alcohol. Or something approaching alcohol. His dad apparently passed down the recipe. It tastes like the last thing you should put in your body and at the rate I'm drinking it, it probably will be.

"Cheat! Belle, cheat!" Hector roars.

Belle throws her cards down. "How do you always know?!"

Hector pours her a penalty shot and slides it across the table. "Because you always lie too big!" He grins.

Belle pokes her tongue out at him. Sometimes I imagine them as orbitals. I think they would be good together, but us moon-sitters aren't supposed to be interested in that sort of thing. They asked us about that when we applied: did we want to get starbound? Did we intend on having children?

Belle slams the shot back and hisses. "Oh, Stars, it's like drinking actual fire."

"Maybe that's his secret ingredient." I laugh.

"No, it's the spiced sauce I keep spiking her shot glass with."

Belle's eyes widen. "You piece of – "

"I'm joking! I'm joking, Belle! Sweet Supernova, calm down!"

I chuckle to myself and slide a mob card, along with a wood card I don't need, facedown onto the table. "Two wood cards for the price of one food card," I state.

"See, Belle, Lucky here knows how to lie small. But, of course, trying to slip it past me while we're arguing is another big giveaway," Hector explains. "Grazer-shit."

I sigh and toss my cards into the discard pile. "Gashole."

"What? I wasn't about to let you mob poor Belle. She's drunk enough."

"I can protect myself, thanks," she grumbles.

Hector splashes the cloudy alcohol into my glass and I try not to let it hit my tongue on its way to my oesophagus. Unfortunately, it hits the back of my throat and triggers a coughing fit.

"Unlucky, Lucky." Hector nudges me with his elbow, then puts four cards in the centre of the table. "Four labour teams for the price of two food."

"Liar! There's no way you have enough labour to go trading it!" Belle roars and flips the cards over. Four labour cards stare up at her. "Are you kidding me?!"

"I told you. I don't lie big." He fires another shot across the table to her. "You should *really* slow down."

Belle scowls and hands him a food card as an apology. I'm still coughing a little.

"Can we take a break? Think I could use some fresh air," I ask.

"Sure. Need to hit the head anyway." Hector stands and strides towards my bathroom.

I walk over to the cabin door and kick it open. Outside, the deck is almost in complete darkness. A string of tiny lights mark the cabin door and another traces the railing either side of the stairs down to the beach. Above, distant stars attempt to sprinkle the land with light, but the Moon blocks out half the night sky. I lean against the wall, slide down it and cross my legs. Belle steps out and takes a seat next to me.

"You okay?" she asks.

"Yeah. I got a little breathless and my head, you know."

"Oh, I know." She smiles.

I stare off at the Moon. She's still looking at me. I can feel her gaze.

"What?"

"Are you still having the dreams?"

I frown. "Of course I am. Can we not talk about it tonight?"

"Sorry. It's just, last night … I thought I saw you out on the beach."

I look at her, startled. "What?"

"Didn't you go for a run last night?"

"No."

"I thought maybe you were trying to clear your head of …" Belle gestures at the Moon.

I shake my head. "I didn't go out last night, Belle."

She shrugs. "Maybe it was Hector."

"Maybe what was Hector?" He grins as he saunters out.

"I thought I saw someone running on the beach last night."

Hector looks concerned. He turns to me. "It was you, Lucky."

I shake my head again. "No. I finished my usual scans and got an early night last night. It was my computer's cool-off night."

"But I saw you run past the new beach monitor."

"Well it can't have been me, because I was in bed. Asleep." My skin is crawling. I stand up and go back inside. I head straight for the alcohol and pour myself a double dose.

"Lucky, do you think you're sleepwalking?" Belle asks. "It could explain why your dreams are so – "

"What dreams?"

I growl. "Thanks, Belle."

Hector has his head tilted to one side. I'm not convinced he's drunk any of his own brew. I think this whole card game was rigged.

"I have these nightmares about running to the Moon …" I begin.

The next thing I know, we're having a sleepover, so they can watch what I do.

I'm in the cabin. The light is red. The walls are singing. When I open the door this time, a wind hits me. I almost fall over, but manage to catch hold of the door frame. When I look at the Moon, it's already dazzling. Now that I think about it, I think it's been getting brighter every night.

I jog down to the beach, noting that Belle's beat-up solarcart is parked next to the staircase. It's odd, but I ignore it and continue towards the jetty. The wind is howling past my ears, yet the water is still perfectly flat, like glass. When I peer in, my reflection remains missing. However, this time, I see the faces of Hector and Belle. I look up at the empty space beside me. They're not there. Something weird is going on, but I feel the pull of the Moon and know I can't stop any longer. I stand up and I start running.

I keep my eyes fixed on the pontoon. I daren't risk looking up for fear that the Moon will blind me. I push through the light. I push through the wind. I feel my heart pound in my chest, I feel my skin begin to peel, I feel the vibration begin to gather in my skull, but I keep running.

When I reach the base of the Moon, I turn around. I can't look at it. I stand there with my back basking in the red glow. I can't see the shoreline. I can barely make out the edge of the pontoon and the vaguely darker shade of the water. Everything is light.

I inch my feet backwards until I feel my heels reach the end of the floating pier. For some reason, I don't throw up. I don't even feel sick. I reach backwards and feel the Moon's smooth cold surface beneath my palm. The noise comes, the waves come, but I remain in place. And then the light begins to fade.

As my eyes adjust, I see that I am standing on all that is left of the jetty. The water is moving again, floating me towards the shore. I sit down and wait to reach the beach. As I sit, I think to myself that none of this is right. None of this feels like it should.

I step onto the sand and it is warm with morning light. That's not right either. Morning light doesn't hit this side of the Moon at this time of year. I spin.

The Moon is gone and Infinity's golden sun shines brightly across my face.

I wake up panting.

"Hector!" I yell. "Belle!"

My mouth doesn't taste like salt water, but my body is buzzing. I tear across my quarters and rip open the curtains. Relief fills me. The Moon is still there, exactly where I left it.

Why am I relieved? I shake my head and wait for guilt to stir. Then try to pretend I don't notice when I feel nothing. *Where are Belle and Hector?*

I knock the door to the bathroom and, after getting no reply, I open it. No-one. I step out onto the deck and walk over to the railing. It's still quite dark, but I can make out a couple of torches and two figures standing on the beach.

I dash back into the cabin and pull on some warmer clothing. I notice the clock says it's six AM.

What are they doing up so early?

They spot me as I reach the bottom of the stairs, where I note Belle's cart exactly where it had been in my dream. I see Belle point at me; her torch flicks into my eyes momentarily. Hector throws his hands up in the air. By the time I reach them, they are stood a good few feet away from each other, not looking at each other and not talking.

"What's going on?"

"I'm not explaining it," Hector snaps.

Belle looks at me suspiciously. "What do you remember from last night?"

"Uh. Well, I had the nightmare, but it was different."

"Different how?"

I think about it for a moment. "To start with, there was wind. The moment I came out of the door, I could feel it pushing me back. And then I saw your cart parked where it is, and both your faces in the water. And I didn't feel nauseous, and I didn't drown. I touched the Moon and the pontoon got torn up, but then I just floated back to shore."

"Anything else?"

I breathe in. "The Moon disappeared."

"The Moon disappeared?!" Hector cackles.

"Yeah."

He shakes his head in disbelief. "Do you want to know what actually happened?"

"Hector …" Belle warns.

"No, you were right. She needs to know," he snarls. "To start with, that 'wind' was me trying to get you to go back in the cabin, and you probably saw us in the water because we were looking too, wondering what in the Void you were doing!"

"Oh."

"Then, of course, you suddenly start running full tilt at the Moon, with me trying to keep you back. I tried yelling at you, holding on to you, but you were so strong, and I didn't want to hurt you. Belle ended up getting a tranquiliser because that's all we could think of to slow you down. Fortunately, it did the job, even though you were supposedly asleep."

"I was asleep."

"Sure."

I look at the Moon, thoughtfully. "So, I didn't touch it last night?"

"No! I wasn't going to let you anywhere near that thing."

"But I dreamt that I touched it. And I survived this time." I wiggle the sand between my toes; it's cold.

"You always drown?" Belle asks.

"Yeah. That's why I call them nightmares."

"You didn't drown because we drugged you and put you to bed before you could jump in the ocean," Hector snarks.

I hum. "Or I didn't die because I touched it without looking at it."

"What? You think the Moon is shy?"

"No," I snap back.

"Then what?"

"I don't know! I just dream this shit."

I walk slowly down the beach towards the jetty.

"Where are you going, Lucky?" Belle touches my hand.

I put one foot on the pontoon. "I need to go and look at it. Okay?"

"Not okay. You know we're not supposed to go anywhere near it," Hector states.

"Well, apparently I've broken that rule a fair few times, and whatever superior species made the damn thing has yet to kill me. So, might as well break the rule once more for luck."

"Lucky – " Belle starts.

"Come inside and eat something," Hector interjects.

I hesitate. My stomach is on the verge of growling and it will be a long walk to the Moon.

"Fine," I say, "But you're not going to change my mind." I take my foot off the pontoon and walk back towards the cargo ship.

About six months after I moved in with Marcus, I woke from my usual nightmare to find myself alone in the cabin. In the glow from the computer screen, I could see that Marcus' bed was completely unslept in, and he wasn't in his desk chair either. I got up to check on the

Moon readings, but got distracted by the papers on his desk. More specifically, my attention was caught by the sight of my name on a manila folder. It was written in Marcus' almost illegible scrawl, which I'd taken to calling our secret code (only the two of us could decipher his handwriting). Curious, I slid the file out of the stack and began to flick through in the dim light. When I started reading, I thought it was my progress review:

Lucky shows high intelligence and promising raw talent for computer programming, which is a marvel given that she has only two years' worth of prior training.

But then it took a strange turn:

Unfortunately, she also appears to be suffering from a sleep disorder. This may be due to the psychological impact of proximity to the Moon, or perhaps due to the brain trauma she experienced as a child? Worth checking medical records in more depth for any prior mention.

I frowned. The next collection of papers in the folder was a copy of my medical records, from my arrival in City up to the flu I caught at fifteen. After that was a chart of the number of times I woke in the middle of the night and on what days. I heard the clang of footsteps on deck and shoved the papers back into the file, then the file back into the clutter on the desk.

I threw myself back under my bed sheets. I was being an idiot, I knew that, acting like a child about to be caught reading under the blankets. It was Marcus who should have felt guilty. He'd been studying me, reading through my personal information. *How did he even get hold of my records?*

Marcus opened the door, walked to the computer and typed something in. The machine beeped. He walked over to his bed and sat on the edge of it.

"Lucky, you awake?" he asked.

I didn't answer.

"Good. I'm glad you're asleep. Fourteen nights in a row. You must be exhausted." He paused. "I wish I could help you, you know? But I think I'd only make it worse."

He slumped back onto his mattress. He murmured something else. Something about wishing he still had his doctor around, but his mouth was covered by blankets and I wasn't about to ask him to repeat himself.

I'm sitting on the table with my feet on a chair, eating a bowl of hydrated grains and desiccated insects, while I watch Hector scroll through reams of Moon data. Belle is leaning on the desk next to him, chewing at the edges of a scute on her hand.

"I don't get it," Hector mutters to himself.

"What is it?" Belle says nervously.

He waves her off for a moment, still reading. He said he was only going to check the last month, but I can see his screen, and he's made it to last year.

"You can't find anything, can you?" I say, my mouth half full.

Hector grunts. Belle leans over his shoulder.

"It's had the exact same readings every night?" she asks.

"Yeah. Looks that way. The Moon's a consistent character, I'll give it that much."

I scrape up the last mouthful from my bowl and suck my spoon clean. I barely tasted the food, but at least my stomach feels the right amount of full for some adventure. I stand and move towards my discarded jumper.

"Lucky, you're not still thinking – " Belle started.

"I am still thinking. We're clearly not going to figure out anything from here."

"This doesn't feel right, Lucky." Belle pushes her hand into her abdomen. "Stars, my gut is hurting."

"It's anxiety, Belle." I push my torso into the warm over-layer. Belle is paler than she should be. "Look, do you want to keep chasing me around every night until retirement? Or do you want answers? Because I would like to know why I seem to be magnetised to that thing."

Hector lets out a sigh. "Lucky's right, Belle. We can't let this go on. Maybe just seeing it up close will stop her nightmares."

"Exactly," I say with a grin.

I don't know why, but I'm excited. Seventeen years

I've lived here, but there was never any reason to walk out into the ocean and see the Moon up close. At least no reason for my conscious mind.

"I'm not letting you go alone, though," Hector adds. He levers himself up out of the chair and stretches his back. "I need the walk after sleeping on your floor."

Belle hasn't moved. She's staring at the fist pressed into her stomach, looking immensely uncertain.

"It's okay, Belle. You don't have to come," I say.

She frowns. "It's not that."

"What's up, then?"

"I think … I think I'm going to stay and monitor things from the ship. I can let you know if anything changes with …" She gestures out the window. I realise, for the first time in years, I don't think I've ever heard Belle call the Moon, *the Moon*.

"That's actually a good idea. I've got my com." Hector taps the tatty old radio attached to his belt.

"Good." Belle nods and sits down next to the computer. Hector steps away and Belle slides herself right up to the desk. "For the record though, I still think this is a terrible idea."

"Noted." Hector looks at me. I'm grinning all over. "Oh, feckin' come on," he says and opens the door to the deck.

I don't really remember my early childhood. My parents told me that they found me lying face down at

the side of a dirt road with a nasty crack on the back of
my head. When I came to, I couldn't remember my
name, or where I came from. So they called me Lucky,
and I stayed with them.

It was a long time before we found a home. I
remember walking all day, every day, until my feet felt
like boulders crammed into shoes. My new parents had
radios, though, and their radios kept us hopeful. There
were people just around the corner, calling to us,
waiting for us to come find them.

Crossing the Marshlands was probably the hardest
bit. The mud had the suction power of a black hole in
places, and one wrong foot would result in a lost boot,
or sock, or life. Someone had set out a trail of bright
orange flags to help traverse the swamp, but the path
was narrow and had clearly shifted when the rains
came.

I remember screaming with a mouthful of mud, my
hands the only thing above the surface. Then I woke
up over my father's shoulder. He laughed and said
maybe they should have called me 'Unlucky.'

When we got to City, there were a lot of tests.
Needles, and running, and blowing into a meter. Mum
said they had to check we weren't poorly.

I remember some terse conversations that happened
in the hall outside my room. They couldn't understand
how I'd survived or why I wasn't ill. They couldn't
understand something about my blood, and my scute
pattern didn't make sense either. In the end, they
simply decided I really was 'Lucky.'

My mum had been a teacher and my dad was an

architect, so when City began to reach capacity, they took jobs in the Marshlands. Dad worked with the salvage teams to help drain the land and resurrect the remaining structures. Everyone called it a town, but it was more of a village. Twenty houses, some shops, and a community-hall-cum-school. The doctor they sent ran his practice from his house. His living room was a waiting room, and his office had a big dining table in it. I don't know why I remember that. I think my mother took me there a lot. She was a bit paranoid.

When they started to offer memorial trips to the Moon, my father outright refused. He said he'd die happy having never seen "the thing" with his own two eyes. But my mother said it was important. I guess I was about ten at the time, but I mean … nobody really knows how old I am. Dad wouldn't talk to Mum, but he kissed me and told me to stay lucky. You may have noticed by now that my childhood (and most of my life, for that matter) was a pun-filled one.

The memorial trip was the first time I'd ever travelled by solarflyer and I was so excited. I loved being in the air. I loved being up high. It felt like that was how the world should always be seen. I didn't care about the weird drop in my stomach or the popping in my ears. I yelled with delight. My mother wasn't happy with my wooting, so eventually I stopped, but my face stayed glued to the window.

It took five days to get to the edge of the continent, with two charging stops. I got frustrated whenever we had to land. There was a lot of sitting and waiting, and Mum wouldn't let me explore. The first stop was on a raised flat covered in red moss. I could see the jungle around the edge and I wanted to know if there were any animals living there, but every time I tiptoed away a hand would clamp down on my shoulder and guide me back toward the fleet of aircraft. The second stop was too cold for exploring and it didn't look all that interesting. The landscape was made almost entirely of jagged black rocks that cut into the sky like teeth.

The Moon itself came into view about two hours before landing. It crept over the horizon like a dead sun. I felt my whole body prickle. Mum went dark and quiet. I didn't ask what it was; I knew. As soon as we landed, we started to set up camp on the rocks behind the cargo ship. The trips weren't only about helping Infinity's citizens find peace. They were also about bringing supplies to set up the first moon-sitters: Marcus, Elena and T.

I remember Marcus coming down the old cargo ship ladder with a leap and a bound. He was in his early thirties, with ridiculously long, red hair and bare feet, but was also "ridiculously bright," our pilot remarked as he helped my mother out of the solarflyer. I liked Marcus immediately because his hair was just as red as mine. Kids at school poked fun at me for my locks. They called me a Southy Spook, a Northern Ghoul, or a Dead Edge, which I thought was stupid because while I might have had the hair and the scute pattern, everyone knew the Edgelanders had stark white skin. Mine had always been dark, like almost everyone else who lived at the centre of the continent.

Marcus was clearly a real Edgeland survivor,

though. His skin was so pale it was practically translucent and his scute patterning was minimal, covering only his forehead, cheeks and joints. He stood out in the crowd of City and Marshland folk, but he didn't seem to notice. I wondered how he didn't get swept away when the Moon came. Maybe he'd been visiting City.

"Hello! Hello! Welcome! I hope your journey was good." Marcus grinned.

Mum looked at him with the face she used on Dad sometimes and said, "People died. This isn't a holiday."

"Oh, no, of course not! I've been working on the solarflyer's stabilisation system, you see? Was wondering if I could get a review?" Marcus jumped into the cockpit and hit a button or two.

My mum grunted, "It needs more work."

She grabbed my hand and towed me towards the small group of gathering memorial visitors. When I looked over my shoulder, Marcus was staring at my mother, or maybe me. I couldn't quite tell. I beamed at him and waved. He looked down at the solarflyer console.

That night we held a vigil on the beach. Someone made an enormous bonfire and the smoke smelled delicious on the breeze. We stood and sang the old tunes we could remember. The Moon sat and watched. It didn't care that it had destroyed our homes, killed our friends and our families. It just watched us try to soothe ourselves, without offering any explanation as to why it was there.

We Infinitians sang until we were hoarse, then

retired to bed.

When Mum was fast asleep, I snuck out of the tent and went back to the beach. The bonfire was nearly out, but it was still mustering up a little light and heat. I parked myself nearby and stretched out my legs, letting the waves lick my toes. Then I stared at the Moon.

Eventually, Marcus wandered down onto the beach and plonked himself down next to me. He was nursing a large glass bottle.

"What d'you think of our friend here?" he asked.

"What?"

"The Moon." Marcus waved and took a drink. "What d'you think?"

I frowned. "I don't know. It doesn't make me feel good. All my hairs are standing up."

Marcus picked up my arm so he could see it in the light; it was covered in goose pimples. "That's the cold, kid."

"No," I grumbled, and pulled my arm free. "It started the moment I saw the Moon."

"Huh, then you probably need this more than I do." He offered me a sip from the bottle.

I was curious, so I tried some. It burnt my lips and tongue and I spat it out over the sand. "Stars!" I spluttered.

Marcus laughed. "An interesting expression, that. Where did you hear it?"

I shrugged. "It's something Mum says sometimes when Dad's not around."

"Hmm," Marcus said thoughtfully. "How linguistic

fashions change."

I brought my legs up to my chest and scratched my chin on the hard edge of my knees. After a while I asked, "What d'you think about the Moon?"

Marcus smiled.

"I think it's the reason I'm a long way from home." He took a giant gulp from the bottle. "But the good news is that the alcohol here isn't half bad."

He tapped the bottle against the sharpest piece of horn on his knuckle; Edgelander scutes evolved for brute force and physical protection, not sun-guarding. The bottle made a chink, chink, chink noise as Marcus lost himself in thought.

"Do you know what sitters were?" he asked eventually.

I shook my head, no.

"They were this type of bird that used to live all around the coast of the continent. We think they're extinct now. No-one's seen one since the Moon arrived." He scraped his knuckle across his brow and I held my breath, expecting him to cut himself. I rubbed the scar above my eye where I'd nicked it the year before. "Edgelanders used to use them to know when it was safe to fish, or when to bring the boats back in, because they'd only fly in the hours before a storm. The rest of the time you'd see them sitting in the boughs of trees all along the shore, or once in a while you'd catch one foraging for food in the evenings."

"They sound cool."

"Yeah. We had them in my home town. I always liked them. They had this interesting habit of living in threes."

"Threes?"

"There was a logic to it: one to stay alert and send a warning, one ready to fight and defend, one that's curious and keeps the group moving forward to new resources." He hummed to himself. "We based the moon-sitter setup on them."

"Really?"

"Mhmm. I figure any more than three people here would be too much data, too many instincts and emotions. You only need three metaphorical birds flying in the sky to confirm there's a storm coming."

I nodded, not really understanding why he was telling me all this.

"Anyway, that's enough of my drunken rambling." He dragged himself up and began to stagger back towards the cargo ship. He got a few paces away before he turned and said, "You better come back here someday and help me with this mess. You hear?"

I blinked, stunned. "Why?"

"Because this is as much your problem as it is mine." Marcus hit himself in the diaphragm and let out a belch. "Just promise me you'll come back."

He looked at the Moon, then back at me. His ghoulish face looked so fierce in the bonfire light that I felt like I couldn't say no. So instead I said, "Okay. I promise."

He smiled and nodded to himself. "See you later then, little sister." He disappeared off up the beach, stumbling occasionally in the sand.

It was a weird night, but it stuck with me. And

about ten years later, I fulfilled my promise.

Hector and I walk, and walk, and walk. I begin to regret not grabbing some kind of footguards before we started this little escapade. The jetty surface is supposed to be smooth, but the wind has engrained it with sea salt, which rubs the soles of my feet and makes it harder to grip. To be honest, though, I'm surprised it's still in such good condition. I suppose Marcus and the others did do some renovations before they retired.

Hector is silent. I can't tell if he's annoyed or scared. His hands are stuffed into the pockets of his trousers. His jaw is rigid.

"Can I ask you a question?" I say.

"Go for it."

"What made you become a moon-sitter?"

He lets out a little laugh. "You haven't asked me that in what ... sixteen years?"

"Well, you just growled the last two times I tried."

"But you think I'll respond differently this time?"

"You weren't exactly offering any talking points."

He nods. "Fair enough."

"So?"

"So ..." He takes a breath. "It's not a complicated story. I was skilled in the sciences, so skilled that City fast-tracked my education at their expense. When I got to the end, they gave me two choices, babysit the Moon for thirty years, or work on some top secret shit

36

they had going at Civic Spire, and basically never see daylight again."

"Damn."

"Yup. I figured being able to retire at fifty was better than disappearing into a black hole."

"They really screwed you, didn't they?"

Hector shrugs. "When they gave me the options, yeah, that's what I thought too. But this thing's been pretty quiet. And you and Belle make for alright company. I've heard the scientists in the Spire work in bubbles and barely communicate."

"Heard from who?"

"Elena. Before she left, I was having some doubts that this was what I wanted to do. She said her nephew basically vanished after he took a job at the Spire."

"City is so fucked sometimes, I swear."

"Yeah." He pauses. "So what about you? Why did you come?"

"Oh, uh. I made a promise when I was a kid."

"To who?"

I laugh. "Oh, you know, myself really. I was on one of those memorial trip things and I knew I needed to come back."

"You did one of those? Good grief, Lucky. No wonder you're obsessed with this thing." He swings his arms wide.

It's been forty minutes and we're almost to the end of the pontoon now. The Moon looks like a flat grey wall in front of us. As we near the edge, I see Hector frown.

"What's up?"

"Does that look right to you?"

He points to the end of the jetty and it takes me a second to figure out what he's talking about. In my head, the pontoon always ended a few feet from the surface of the Moon, but in reality it's quite clearly been severed. The edge of the plastic is black and bubbled where something has melted a chunk away. I jog to the end and kneel down to inspect the damage. It's such a neat line that, for a moment, l think someone's cut it off with a blowtorch. Then I realise that there's a slight curve to it.

"Hector, can you get hold of Belle?"

"Already on the line." He hands me the com.

"Hey, Belle, what are the readings coming from the Moon right now?"

"They look normal."

"How about the water? What temperature is it?"

"It's normal for this time of year. About twelve degrees."

I look at Hector. He's as baffled as I am. He extends his hand out to me and I give him back the radio.

"Can you check the data from the last twenty-four hours again?" he asks Belle.

I stand up and look at the Moon. It towers above us, but it's still out of reach. The water below me is dark, but I'm fairly certain there's nothing swimming in it. Every time we've tried to fish these waters, we haven't caught a thing.

Hector turns away, shielding his mouth from the wind as he talks into the radio. He doesn't want to look at the Moon, or the melted pontoon.

I strip off my jumper and joggers and dive into the water before he can stop me. I keep my lips glued tight and hold my nose while the cold water tries to make me gasp.

As I surface, Hector yells, "Lucky! What are you doing?"

I tread water for a moment, trying to get my body to adjust. It takes less time than I expect it to, but then I've always fared well in cold temperatures. "I'm going to go take a look."

"Get back up here now!"

"I'm fine. Nothing's gonna eat me."

"That's not what I'm worried about."

We both look at the Moon.

"You know why I came, Hector, and it's not just to look at it." With that, I start swimming away.

"Lucky!" I hear him yell. "Lucky, I can't swim. Stars, you arse!"

I push my head into the water and swim faster, straight at the Moon. It's not far. I can still hear him yelling when I reach touching distance. I tread water again. It's not glowing, but I can feel a vibration coming from the Moon's surface. My skin is tingling, from toes to scalp.

I think about last night's dream and I spin in the water. Hector is waving at me furiously with one arm. The other is holding the comm near his ear. I listen for a moment, to check he's not yelling anything important, but it's the same message. *Come back, get out of the water.*

I grit my teeth. And then reach one arm up and

back as far as I can manage. There's no heat. So I touch it.

There's a loud noise and a gust of air, but neither are as forceful as they've been in my dreams. I see Hector's arm still and then fall slowly to his side in shock. I turn and see that a hole has appeared in the side of the Moon, tall and rectangular.

It's a door.

The bottom is in reach, so I grab hold and begin to pull myself out of the water. That's when Hector starts shouting again. I stand up on the dark metallic floor and turn to tell him everything's fine. The door slides shut in my face.

I was a curious kid, too curious. I frequently came home with fewer scutes than I'd left with and often found myself stuck up trees. So it's no surprise that my parents felt the need to recite the story of Red Planet to me at least once a week:

> *Red Planet cracked open its chest to find out*
> *what was inside. Abyss reached in and dragged*
> *Core out by the hand. Core breathed in the*
> *nothingness, laughed and ran away. Then Red*
> *Planet cried and cried, for it was soon to die and*
> *had never learnt Core's name.*

I wasn't particularly interested in Red Planet's story,

perhaps because it didn't have a happy ending, like the Moon's tale. I certainly didn't really see how it applied to me at all. That is, until I got lost in the foothills near the Marshland.

I don't know what possessed me, really. I was only eleven. I think I was trying to get around the mountain range for some reason. Something in my gut told me there were interesting artefacts or buried treasure just out of sight. I was also already out in the fields, making grass whistles, so nothing in my body suggested that I should inform my parents where I was going first. That was another nasty habit of mine; whenever I made a decision, I followed it through without consulting anyone.

So yes, I set out on my foothill excursion fully believing I was capable of surviving the hike … without a map … or footguards (I have never been good at remembering to wear them when I need them). I did have some food and water, though. I wasn't that stupid.

About an hour later, everything hurt and I was baking hot. I decided I needed a sit down in the shade, so I hiked up the hill into the trees. We were always told to avoid sitting on the floor in uncultivated zones, so I searched for a bit and found myself a nice boulder. I clambered up, then pulled a sugar-cake and water flask out of my backpack. I sat there for a while, feeling quite pleased with myself as I gobbled up my picnic. *This,* I thought, *was an excellent plan.*

After I'd packed up my things, I decided it was a good idea to stay under the jungle canopy. I didn't want to get hot again; I didn't have a great deal of water left once I'd finished my lunch. Mum and Dad used to say that it was easy to get lost in the jungle, but I was on a hill. I reasoned that if I wanted to get out, I merely had to walk down the slope and I'd come out eventually.

You can imagine the alarm I felt when, after another hour of epic adventure, I suddenly realised that the land beneath my feet had flattened out. Worse still, I couldn't remember when it had gone flat because I'd been too preoccupied chasing an interesting-looking bird through the tangle of vegetation.

"Oh, pissing Void!" I remember cursing, then looking around to see if I'd summoned an adult. Unfortunately, I hadn't.

I looked up at the green and red glow of the canopy, trying to figure out where the sun was, but there wasn't a big enough hole to spot it.

"Well, there's no use panicking," I assured myself. "I'll just have to pick a direction and walk."

So walk I did. I tried, very carefully, to walk in a consistent straight line. Of course, it's almost impossible to do that in a jungle, but at the time I didn't know that and, to be honest, I'm glad I didn't.

Eventually, I started to get really thirsty again, so I drank the rest of my water. Then my stomach let out a gurgle, so I stopped and ate my other sugar-cake. I told myself that I needed the energy now, in order to get home in time for dinner. There was no point saving it.

When the jungle started to go dark, that's when I started to panic. I was lost in an endless sea of trees and

creatures I didn't know the names of. I found myself
another boulder, heaved myself up it and sat there
wide awake for most of the night.

I woke up with the kind of back pain eleven-year-
olds are not supposed to experience. I'd unfurled, so
that I was lying convex over the top of the great rock,
and my body was not pleased. I sat up, mouth dry,
stomach howling in hunger, and sighed. Then I roared
at the top of my voice, "Somebody help me!"

Just like that, a pale man with purplish hair peered
around a tree trunk. I'd never seen anyone so pale
before, but he seemed to know me.

"Hey, kiddo!" He smiled, but for some reason his
face was a blur. I could only make out the warmth of
his grin.

"H-hi," I said. "I'm lost."

"Really? How'd you manage that?"

"I walked too far and I didn't bring a map and a map
wouldn't help anyway because all I've seen is jungle,
jungle, jungle."

"Stars, that's not good." His smile disappeared,
replaced instead by the image of a furrowed brow.

"Can you help me?" I pleaded.

The smile returned. "Oh, yes! Of course."

The purple-haired man reached out his hand. He
was wearing strange clothes, but he seemed nice
enough, so I let him help me down and then followed
him.

"You know, kid. You really shouldn't wander so far
from home."

"I know."

"Even if your mum and dad don't always seem to do what's right, they love you. You know that, don't you?"

I looked up at his blurry face in confusion. "What do you mean? Mum and Dad always do what's right. Sometimes it's annoying."

He smiled weakly and nodded. "Okay."

We walked for hours, but he pointed out little animals and flowers and he knew the names for all of them.

"A lot of these things travelled a very long way to live here," he said.

"Why'd they do that?" I asked.

"Oh, people brought them when they first settled here."

"Mum and Dad didn't bring anything."

"No, but they weren't the first to come."

"You're weird," I stated. He was talking nonsense. Clearly he'd been in the jungle alone for too long. Maybe the Marshland doctor could give him a pill or something.

Eventually, we started to hear voices. They were quiet at first, and I couldn't make out what they were saying, but then one deep booming voice that I instantly recognised as my father yelled, "Lucky!"

"Dad!" I shouted back.

"Lucky?!"

"Over here!" I turned to my pasty white guide and beamed at him.

"Why are they calling you Lucky?" he asked.

"It's my name," I said, then yelled again. "I'm over here, Dad!"

My father barrelled through the undergrowth and wrapped his arms around me. "You menace. We've been searching for you since lunchtime yesterday," he huffed into my shoulder. "You had us so worried, Lucky."

"I'm sorry, Dad. I promise I won't ever do this again."

He put me at arm's length and checked over my body. "Are you hurt anywhere?"

"No," I answered. "Just really hungry and thirsty. I thought I'd be home by dinner."

He pressed his armoured forehead against mine. "Blast, girl! Be glad I love you." He squeezed my arms tightly, then stood up. "Come on, it's still a trek home, but we brought enough supplies to keep looking for you all day."

I smiled, then turned to introduce my purple-haired friend.

"This is – " I started, but the pale man was gone.

"What's that?"

"There was a man, with white skin and purple hair. He helped me find you."

My dad looked at me like I was crazy. "I think you need water, fast."

"No, really."

"Lucky," Dad said, towing me out of the jungle, "White men with purple hair don't exist."

45

I breathe. I'm alone, in the dark, inside the Moon,
having a quiet flashback to that night in the jungle. But
everything is fine because my lungs are still working
and that's what's important. I spin to face the centre of
the giant sphere and press my back against the wall.
Then I slide, feeling my way around. Suddenly the
ceiling bursts into light and I feel like I've gone blind. I
blink rapidly, trying to get my eyes to adjust.

A hall, long and black and sparkling, stretches away
from me. The ceiling is entirely light; It gives a strange
red hue to the whole place. I take a moment to check
that I'm still alone. There's no-one that I can see, but
the hallway seems endless. I step away from the wall.
When I glance over my shoulder, I realise my hand had
been pressed against a silver panel. I touch it again and
the whole room plunges into darkness, then again to
bring the light back.

"Why can I do that?" I say to myself.

I spot another panel, on the other side of where the
open door once was. When I touch it, nothing happens.
I think about how I never really learnt my lesson as a
kid. I'm still too curious.

*Dad would kill me if he knew where I was right
now.*

Unable to get out, I take a walk down the corridor.
From time to time I see another silver panel. Some of
them turn the lights on and off, but most of them seem
to be dead.

Maybe guests only get to mess with the lighting?

I push on. My legs begin to ache and I realise that, if
I'm walking to the centre of the Moon, the journey will

take me at least another forty minutes at this pace. I consider turning back, but I'm already past the halfway point.

If I turn back now, there's no way Hector and Belle are going to let me do this again.

I might not even let myself do this again.

Sometime later I come to a large circular room. When I step in, the wall closes behind me. For some reason, I don't feel claustrophobic; I'm not panicking at all. The way the floor and walls glitter makes me think of the stars on the ceiling of my cabin.

I take a few paces into the room. There's a pedestal in the centre with a glass orb perched on top. As a kid, Mum used to tell me never to touch the stuff on pedestals in City museum and, as I reach to touch the orb, her voice rings in my ears. Still, my gut is telling me to press my hand against it, because that seems to be how this place works.

I put my hand on the glass and a projection flickers into life above me. I do a double take at the face that appears; it's Marcus.

He stares into the recording device for a moment. From the wrinkles around his eyes, I guess he's coming up on forty. His forehead plate looks a little damaged, redder, as if burnt. The recording must be from before I arrived. He cracks his jaw and pulls at the stubble on his chin.

"Hi, Lucky," he sighs. His head sinks. "If you're seeing this, then I guess you made it into the Moon. Maybe you haven't forgotten as much as I hope. Maybe you remember what I did … I don't know. But if you've made it here, I guess you're not going to stop looking for answers, even if you don't remember any of it. So I'd better explain, before you go making things worse."

He turns and picks something up. It's a bottle. Now I think about it, it's odd. In the ten years I lived with Marcus, I never once saw him touch a drop of alcohol. But here he is on some recording, getting drunk and talking to me once again, just like when I was a kid.

"Right. Let's start with this. You're not gonna like it, and maybe you'll struggle to believe it, but you're not from Infinity, Lucky. Neither am I. You and I fell out of the Moon when it landed." He drinks. "Oh, Stars, what am I doing?" He claws at his face. "This is a ridiculous plan …"

I'm standing with my hand still pressed against the orb. I feel hot. Hot all over. I swallow hard.

Marcus sighs. "The Moon is actually a colony ship. It's designed to travel to an uninhabited planet, land, and then begin a terraforming process. Meanwhile, the colonists on board are kept in stasis, asleep, until the world is liveable.

"I don't really know what happened. From what I can tell, the ship malfunctioned. It chose an already inhabited planet, then failed to release the colonists. Only a handful of stasis pods were jettisoned and only the two of us survived."

My next breath tastes like ice and smoke. The world is spinning.

"We didn't land all that far from each other. You found me crying over my orbital's body. He was covered in blood and starting to feel cold. I was so grief-stricken, I thought I was imagining you, but eventually you started to get hungry and then you were crying because I wouldn't leave and you thought we were both going to die."

I kneel down on the floor, hand still on the orb, and lean the side of my face against the cool pillar. Marcus' voice continues.

"We must have walked for days. And there was no food. And no people. And no way of signalling for help. You were starving. You could barely move. I didn't know what to do. So, so I …"

My eyes are closed, but I can hear the sound of him knocking back whatever swill it is he's drinking. He takes a deep breath. I take one too and hold it.

"I tried to do what was best. I didn't want you to suffer anymore. I … I hit you over the head and left you to die."

I collapse down onto the floor and the recording stops. I pull my arms tight to my chest. My body feels like it's on fire, like the whole world is burning, and my knuckles are digging into the flesh of my arms. Marcus was wrong. So wrong. I'm not struggling to believe him, because as he says the words, the memories play out in my head, crystal clear. My head is pounding.

I lie on the floor for a long time, trying to find the edges of myself and knit them back together. Somehow, I find the strength to pull myself upright against the pedestal. I reach up, and Marcus' face reappears in the air.

"I don't know what to say. Since the day you turned up on the solarflyer, the day I realised you were still alive, I've done nothing but think about what I could say. Nothing works. Nothing makes up for trying to murder a kid. The best I can manage is … sorry."

There are tears in his eyes. I know he means it, but I can't help thinking he's a coward for not doing this in person. He had ten years, ten whole years where pulling me aside to have a quiet word about our tragic backstory would have taken nothing more than a, "Hey, Lucky. Come here a sec."

He grunts, as if he knows what I'm thinking and mutters, "I'm such a piece of shit."

Then he wipes his whole arm across his face and continues.

"After I left you, I continued walking and found City. I stole a name, made up a life. I told them I was from a forested area in the mountains, that I'd lost my orbital in a rock slide and had been wandering, distraught. They believed me, they had no reason not to, and it wasn't a total lie. I've always been a dab hand with technology, so I quickly found myself in demand. Then, soon enough, I found I was able to make demands. My first request was that we set up stations to monitor the Moon. The Infinitians thought it was a sensible suggestion; make sure the Moon wasn't going to do anymore damage. Me, I wanted to know what had happened to our people.

"But it doesn't really matter how I got here. Or how you got here. We're just here, back where we started."

We blink at each other.

"I wish you hadn't made it this far, Lucky. I don't know. It probably would have been better if you'd died in that ditch." He growls at himself. "I don't mean it like that. But, you see, we're all going to die soon enough. The Moon is as inert as I could make it, but it's still switched on and the sensors are broken. From the moment it landed, it started trying to terraform the planet, Lucky. And there's no way to stop it."

I snap my hand away from the orb and stand up. I've had enough. Okay, some of what he's saying I know to be true; I can feel the memories continuing to crawl their way back into my consciousness like a thousand mites. But any machine can be stopped. I'm not going to be told I'm about to die. Marcus might be defeated, but I'm not.

I look for other panels, other indents. I try to remember being on this ship before.

What makes the Moon tick?

This seems central enough to be a control room, but there don't appear to be any controls other than the orb. I sigh. If Marcus didn't want me to make anything worse, there's a good chance he's jerry-rigged the orb to play the video, so I can't access anything until I've heard what he has to say. It wouldn't be the first time he's tried to stop me accessing important information.

When I get back to my cabin, that gashole is getting a piece of my mind.

I start pawing at the pedestal, hoping to find a loose panel, or a switch, but I can't see anything. I get a terrible feeling that the only way forward is through. I put my hand back on the orb and grit my teeth.

"The Moon was finishing up its first scans when I finally reached it. This tin can didn't pick up any life signs on Infinity. Not one. If I'd rocked up a couple of days later, then boom! We'd all be fertiliser for a new homeworld right now.

"Fortunately, I managed to disrupt its programming and reroute some power, but some genius put in a failsafe. When the power drops to a certain level, the Moon will lock me out and start running all the terraforming programmes it can.

"In the meantime, this ship keeps bucking like a bloody grazer, occasionally starting random procedures. Even the fish and the birds know this area isn't safe. Last night I caught the stupid thing about to boil the ocean clean. It took a great chunk off the end of the jetty before I could stop it. I imagine you saw that on the way in.

"I'm telling you, Lucky, the damn Moon will kill off everything soon enough. I can control the damage from here for now, and maybe when I retire I can rig something up, keep an eye on it from the Spire. But when the Moon reaches that minimum power requirement, it will overwrite every command I give it. It will … it will …"

I crack the knuckles on my free hand. He's drunk and rambling and I want him to get on with it, so I can actually find a way to fix the problem.

He coughs. Puts down his bottle.

"Okay. Right. You're an alien, check. I tried to kill you, check. We're all going to die, check. What have I forgotten?" He frowns to himself. "Oh. Right." He

52

makes a popping sound with his mouth. "I did think of one way to turn this shit off for good, but the only way to do it is to kill every single person currently asleep in the Moon." He nods to himself. "Yeah. They'd all have to die, because then the Moon would shut down. It wouldn't have any cargo to terraform for, see? And before you say, 'Can't we release them all?' only the captain can authorise that now, and while it might be possible to release him from stasis early, his location on the ship was not disclosed to anyone outside of the family travelling with him. Not to mention, his quarters are probably genetically protected. So, yes, either everyone on the planet dies, or everyone on the Moon dies. That's the choice. And I can't live with it any longer, Lucky. So, I guess that really does make me a piece of shit, because it's your decision now. Which'll it be? Infinity or the Moon?"

The video disappears, but control units rise up from the floor, their panels lighting up the room. Above me, in the space where Marcus' head had been, a shimmering blue countdown appears; I have eighteen hours until the Moon tears apart everything on the surface of Infinity. The control room door opens. I taste something metallic in my mouth and realise I've bitten my tongue so hard it's bleeding. I spit at the countdown, at Marcus, and start to jog back to the Moon's exit.

I've always had this vague memory of running through a field on a planet with an amber sky. I thought it was a dream, but now I know I'm not from Infinity, I know that the memory is real. My mind is working overtime, hammering together scraps I hadn't even thought to connect. And the clarity is absurd, like I'm living it all over again.

I wasn't running through any old field. Space shuttles loomed above me, their great white spires piercing the sky. They looked so tall I was afraid they would topple over and crush me and my family. I wanted to tiptoe through, but my birth mother and biological father were jogging along next to me, two white-skinned giants pushing me forward. Both of them were carrying huge duffle bags full of our belongings. They'd explained to me that we were going to a new planet, with a pretty blue sky, but I didn't want to go. I liked our red sun and orangey atmosphere. As we ran, Dad let out an extra loud grunt and scooped me up. He slung me over his free shoulder and I was instantly winded by his enormous plate of shoulder scutes. I let out a cry.

"Shh, we're almost there."

His shoulder bounced me up and down, pushing the air from my lungs with every stride he took. Mum saw that I was in pain and gave me an empathetic smile.

Five minutes later, the earth beneath my father's feet was replaced by metal and he plonked me down. Mum and Dad both breathed sighs of relief and grinned at each other. I pulled up my shirt and rubbed my belly. My pale, white belly.

Dad bent and kissed my forehead. "Sorry, but we were running late. And you know I can't be late."

I nodded.

"Once we're in orbit, get Doc to have a look," he said to my mother.

I grinned. I loved Uncle Doc. I can't recall his face now, but I know I loved him. The lift swept up and my stomach churned. Mum frowned.

"Maybe I should take her now?" she asked.

My dad glanced at his time piece. "Launch is in thirty minutes. They'll want everyone strapped in in twenty. I imagine Doc's already dosed himself. He'll be useless for the next hour."

Mum rolled her eyes. "Why did he even sign up for this?"

"You know wherever his orbital goes, he goes too."

"Same here," Mum said with a wink.

We stepped out of the lift and started down the corridor. The interior of the shuttle was as sparse and white as the exterior, but then it was designed for function, not comfort. Dad read off the family names until he found one marked "Moonlight". It wasn't our name, but he pressed his hand against a silver panel next to the door and it slid open. Inside was a small table with three padded jumpseats.

"Right, bags in here for now." Dad touched a panel on the wall and a storage compartment slid open.

"Can I have my dinosaur?" I asked. I wanted something to hold on to. I'd been in a number of simulators over the past year and I hated all of them. The rumbling, the noise, the way my stomach rocked and rolled. I didn't pass out as much anymore, but I always threw up. That was deemed acceptable progress for a child passenger.

"After the launch. We don't want him hurting someone during take-off."

"Okay."

Dad pushed his bag into the compartment first, then Mum placed hers on top. I struggled to imagine how all of our things fit into those two bags.

"Right, find your seat. I want to see you strap and unstrap yourself while we have gravity."

I pouted, but followed Dad over to the table. Each jumpseat had a name and position carefully engraved into the headrest: Dr. Lyra Starling (Genetic Re-coder, 1st Class), Nova Starling (Child, Class C/W.6), Saros Starling (Admiral of Fleet, Captain of the *Ofurion*). I ran my fingers over the engravings, then turned the seat marked "Nova" and climbed into it.

"Excellent, Nova!" Dad clamped a hand onto the back of the chair to keep it facing him. "Can you remember why it's important that you always sit in this seat?" he asked as I buckled myself in.

"Each seat is built special. I'm small, so I need less air in emergencies."

"Now, quickly, what checks do you need to do before take-off?"

"Buckle, padding, mask and eject," I said, and undid my belt to finish my demonstration.

"Good girl. Right." He turned to my mother. "I have to go check-in to the control room now, but I'll be back once we've breached the atmosphere."

Mum nodded. "Fly safe."

He laughed. "Safer than I ever have before."

I'm the daughter of the guy in charge of the Moon. My real name is Nova. That's who I really am.

Fucking Stars.

When I reach the end of the sparkling corridor, I can hear banging on the Moon's hull. I press my palm to the previously dead silver panel and this time the door slides open. Hector and Belle are in an emergency raft, both holding a hammer and chisel set. They look up at me in surprise.

"Hey."

"Lucky! Shining shit! Are you alright?" Belle garbles.

"Yeah," I say.

Hector is looking at me with marked intensity. I sit down on the edge of the door way and close my eyes. I feel a hand touch my knee.

"Lucky?"

I jerk my leg so the hand moves away.

"Look. I've, uh, I've got some news. Some big news, but I need to talk to Marcus, okay?"

"What happened in there? You've been gone for almost three hours."

I crack my fingers. Belle winces. Hector frowns. I begin clicking my tongue, fidgeting with the smooth surface of the ship interior, then pounding it with my fist.

"Oh, fuck it!" I yell. "I'm not from Infinity, alright? I'm an alien! The Moon is a pissing colony ship and if I don't talk to Marcus we're all going to get terraformed into oblivion in less than sixteen hours."

Belle begins to laugh, then looks at Hector and realises he's not smiling. "Are you for real?"

I grind my fist into the edge, where the floor meets the hull, leaving a fine white line of ground horn from my knuckles. "Yes."

"You can't be. You look just like us. I mean, your skin tone, hair colour and scute combo have always been a bit unique, but I figured one of your biological parents was an Edgelander," Belle rambles nervously.

"Well, they weren't. In fact, I'm fairly certain my bio folks are on this thing somewhere." I point over my shoulder into the black cavern.

There's a silence filled with ocean waves and the dull hum of the Moon. Hector taps my knee.

"Look at me, Lucky," he says.

Lifting my head feels awkward and unnatural, but I somehow manage to meet his gaze.

"You planning an invasion?" he asks. He's shaking all over, but there's a twinkle in his eye.

"No."

"Then get in the boat." He smiles softly.

I drop down from the Moon and the entrance closes. Hector hands me the clothes I left on the pontoon and I wriggle back into them. Belle steers us to shore. She doesn't look at me again the whole way. Hector glances at me a few times, and when I catch him he gives me a measured smile. None of us speak. The moment we reach the shallows, I jump out of the boat and jog through the water, kicking up waves with my heels. The sand sticks to my feet. The rocks scrape it off again. I race up to the deck of my cargo ship and into the cabin. My comm is tucked down the side of my computer's housing, so it takes a moment to dig out.

"Moon-Sitter 1 to City, come in, please," I pant into the receiver.

"This is City, what can we do for you, Moon-Sitter 1?"

"I need to speak to former resident Marcus. It's urgent."

"Have the Moon's signals changed?"

I look at my screen. They spiked while I was inside, but they're back to normal range. I debate whether to echo this message down the line. I don't want to cause alarm.

"No," I say. "Tell him, tell him it's about our residence. I've remembered the problem and I need his help to fix it."

"What is the problem?"

I sigh and think for a moment. "The sensors aren't measuring temperature properly. It's causing false life-sign pings."

"Why would you forget that?"

"I caught some weird data before my last trip to City, but I didn't have chance to look into it properly."

"That seems poor practice, Moon-Sitter 1."

"Can I just talk to Marcus, please?!"

"He's in a meeting."

I growl audibly. "Then drag him out!"

"Moon-Sitter 1, this hardly seems like an emergency. The other moon-sitting venues have their own temperature sensors, which I assume are functional?"

"Look, City, I don't have time for this. The matter I have to discuss with Marcus is private and urgent. Get him out of that meeting and place this comm in his hands, right now!"

"Moon-Sitter 1, you know this comm channel is not meant for personal use."

"City, you know that I will, in all seriousness, hunt you down and kill you with my bare hands?"

"Are you threatening me, Moon-Sitter 1?"

"Stars ... well, it's an empty threat, because if you keep dicking around I'll probably be dead before I can get to you."

"Dead? Do you require medical attention?"

"No! I require the attention of former resident Marcus."

"Hello, Lucky?" a familiar voice interjects.

"Councilman Marcus?" City asks, startled.

"Yes. City, please disconnect yourself from this call, immediately," Marcus replies.

"Yes, sir."

There is a click as the comms officer hangs up.

"I'm sorry about that, Lucky. They decided to put you on speaker and laugh about it in the comms room. You know what they think of moon-sitters. We're all crackpot hermits. Anyway, I could hear you from the board room."

"Shit. Did they hear what I was saying?"

"No, thankfully. But I could tell it was you. I slipped into the office next door to take the call."

"Good. Thank you. I mean fuck you, but also thank you."

"Ah," Marcus falls silent. In the space of two words, he already knows that I know. It's not a massive leap of logic. "How long have we got left?"

I chew my tongue for a moment, debating whether to tear him a new one, or shoot straight for the problem. Heroism manages to win, somehow. "Around fifteen hours."

I hear him sigh, "Idiot," quietly to himself.

My jaw tightens. I don't have time for his self-pity. "Right. You said there's no way to turn it – the Moon, the *Ofurion*, whatever you want to call it – off that you can see? Because it's broken? And the only way to stop it completely is to either get everyone in the Moon out of stasis or kill them all in their sleep."

He swallows. His reply comes out in one long sigh of resignation, "Correct, but we can't take everyone out of stasis because we're not the captain."

"Okay, well, what if I told you I'm Nova Starling?"

"You're who now?!"

"I've remembered my real name. It's Nova, Nova Starling. I boarded with my mother, Lyra, and father, Fleet Admiral Saros Starling."

I hear a pounding noise, Marcus hammering whatever desk he's at with excitement. "So you know where their pods are?"

"Things are coming back to me. I can probably find

61

them. But if I ejected …"

"Then they might have. Which means they're probably dead," he finishes without pause.

"Thank you."

"Apologies, old Urion habits die hard." The name of my homeworld slips off his tongue and slots into my memory like it's always been there; Er-ri-un. "We're a straight-talking species. But, yes, there's no way Saros would have hidden for so long. If he was awake and alive, he'd have made it back to the Moon years ago."

I cough. I know he's right. Both Marcus and myself found our way to the Moon. Even if my biological father was wandering around in a fugue state, one glimpse of the Moon would have been enough to lure him home.

"How do I get up to the stasis pod level?"

"Lucky …"

"It's worth trying, isn't it? If it could save both races?"

"Of course." I hear the smile in his voice.

"Then I'm going to make the decision you couldn't, Marcus. Everyone is going to live today. And then the next time I see you, I'm going to punch you in the throat."

"Understandable," Marcus mutters. "But there's one more thing you should know, Lucky."

"What?"

"If you find your father, if he's still there, the emergency release may not work. I've tried other pods, and I couldn't get them open."

"So even if I find him, we might still be screwed?"

"Not entirely. You see, you only really need his hand to activate the cargo release."

The launch was as rough and as horrible as I expected. Pushing the enormous shuttle into orbit took a vast amount of thrust. Even with stabilisers, I threw up and then passed out. My mother roused me once we were in orbit. She wiped my face and gave me a tube of gel hydration. I remember loving that stuff. We'd started replacing our diet with space recommended products about two months before the launch. I quickly became addicted to squirting gel into my mouth, where it would melt into cool water. I've never considered myself a particularly nostalgic person, but for some reason the memory of gel hydration makes my chest warm.

After reaching orbit, we had a few hours of recovery time. My dad radioed to say he was busy in the control centre, ensuring the ship was ready to dock with the *Ofurion's* port, and would meet us at our quarters before disembarkation began. Mum helped me out of my seat, then dragged me to the shuttle's small medical bay. There weren't many people there. Most of the shuttle's human cargo were adults, so it was just me, Mum and a couple of other parents with green-looking children. I remember Uncle Doc's purple hair was sticking up all over. Apparently he'd been busy taking inventory before the launch and hadn't noticed the time until the instructions to buckle in echoed through the intercom. We both smelled vaguely of vomit as he poked and prodded my abdomen. I'm surprised neither of us threw up again. He declared my stomach slightly bruised and packed me off with a mild pain med. An Urion with long red hair threw the med spray over his shoulder at my mother. He didn't even look. Mum exchanged a look with Uncle Doc and Doc went red, right to the tips of his ears.

After that, Mum and I went back to our quarters to wait. We played dinosaur tea party, reptile rampage and soar-o-saur, but still, we didn't dock. Mum told me to take a nap. I was tired, so I let her plug me back into my jumpseat, as long as I could hold onto my dino.

I was drifting in and out of consciousness when I heard Mum hit the room com.

"This is Lyra Starling," she said. "I was wondering if my husband is available?"

"One moment."

"Lyra?" My dad's voice echoed through the com.

"Hey. Is everything's alright?"

My dad let out a sharp burst of laughter. "Not exactly. The good news is that *Ofurion* has apparently located an ancient, lost satellite. The bad news is that it's now stuck, blocking the docking unit. And, of course, Celeste isn't where he should be. If he'd gone with the group last month, they would have shifted it already. But no, the great Aerglo Celeste couldn't possibly leave Urion soil without his orbital. I've never known an engineer to be so thoroughly illogical. Still, we should be moving soon."

"Okay. Is there anything I can do to make things go faster? Perhaps talk to – "

"Oh, no. Don't get Celeste involved now. He'll only throw a fit I didn't call for him earlier. How's Nova?"

"Slightly bruised, but sleeping."

He sighed. "I hope her skin toughens up soon. She'll need it where we're going."

"I'm sure it will. She has your complexion, and your skin is practically impenetrable."

My dad chuckled softly. "Red hair, white skin …"

"Strong as steel, born to win," Mum sang back to him.

"Mmm. Of course, that new pigment gene will kick in when we get there."

"She'll still have your armour, Saros."

"That's the theory."

"Do you doubt my team?"

"No, my wonderful orbital. The Stars and your mother's sample blessed you with a great deal of talent."

"Exactly. So trust that Nova will be just as dangerous as her father," my mother joked, and they both chuckled. "I'll see you soon, Saros."

Hector and Belle reach the cabin door as I exit. I storm past them in a pair of heavy-duty footguards, a machete tied around my waist and a sledgehammer swinging in my hands. I don't want to talk. I don't want to listen. I want to get back to the Moon and get this over with.

"Lucky?"

I laugh. *Why, why, why did anyone ever think it was a good idea to call me that?*

"What, Isabelle?" I say, still walking.

They're following me. I wish they wouldn't. I wish they'd leave me alone to my new life of alien melodrama.

"Where are you going?"

"Back to the Moon."

"Why?"

"I don't want to talk about it."

Hector grabs my arm and pulls me to a stop. The sledgehammer swings and narrowly misses his knee. "Lucky, look, I get it. Whatever this is, it's messed up! But you need to slow down, tell us what's happening and let us help."

"Do I?" I reply. "Do I need to let you help me break a stasis pod, kill my father and cut off his hand, so that I can stop the Moon from terraforming the planet into oblivion? Because that's what I'm probably going to have to do. That's the current situation."

"What?" Belle laughs.

"My bio-dad is the admiral or captain of that." I point at the Moon. "The only way to stop the sodding thing from killing everyone is to release him from stasis, but if the release is broken – which it likely is – I'm going to have to kill him and use his hand to unload the Moon's entire cargo." I'm practically foaming at the mouth. I'm surprised that what I'm saying is even coherent at this point.

Belle gapes at me. "This is ... I'm sorry, but I'm out. This is unbelievable." She shakes her head. "You two are pulling some shitty prank and I'm done here."

She holds up her hands and starts to walk up the beach in the direction of her solarcart. Hector looks at her, then at me. He grabs my other arm, and suddenly I'm being embraced. I stiffen in his arms. We are both shaking.

I can't cry. I won't cry. I need to get back to the Moon. I need to get this over with. I squirm. Hector lets go.

"I'm sorry," he says. "It's hard to know how to ... you know?"

I nod. "You're telling me."

Then I turn and walk toward the emergency raft. I feel Hector behind me. I don't understand why. You'd think that discovering a friend is part of an alien race that accidentally killed most of the life on your planet, and is now accidentally going to kill the rest of it, would send a person running. Apparently not Hector. But then Hector has always been the protective one. He can't help himself. Even when I decided to investigate the blocked off areas of the cargo ship, he had to come with me.

I shove the boat back into the water, then climb in. Hector follows. I steer us back to the Moon, touch the metal panelling and the great sphere slides open again. I throw the machete in ahead of me, pull myself up onto the black floor. Then Hector passes up the hammer. He hesitates before reaching out his hand so I can help him inside. *So he is scared.*

The lights are already lit. As I stand up, I note how different it feels the second time around. In the back of my mind, I know it's a giant death trap, but for a moment the Moon feels like home. A quick flicker of my habitation on Urion hits me. Maybe Saros had a hand in the Moon's interior design.

Hector is silently observing the hallway. He catches my eye. "Nice place you have here." He smiles nervously.

I frown. "Yeah. Well. It's alright."

"Where are we going?"

I point down the hallway and start walking. "Marcus said there's an elevator three doors down."

"Marcus?"

"Yeah."

"Oh. That makes sense!"

I look at him curiously. "What makes sense?"

"You're both aliens, right?" I nod. He continues, "It's just you're the only two red-haired folk I've ever met. Elena once told me she'd never seen anyone with hair as red as you or Marcus, and her grandmother was an Edgelander."

I blink.

"Sorry, that probably sounds kind of bigoted or something."

"No ... maybe a bit, but it's nothing."

Hector's not wrong. My hair is almost a perfect shade match to Marcus'. And our scute patterns are practically identical. Saros looked much the same. Lyra had the same patterning, but darker, purplish hair. I pinch the flesh of my arm thoughtfully, remembering how translucent it was on Urion. I wonder how and when it turned so dark.

"You okay?"

"Yeah … I'm just remembering things that don't make much sense."

"Like what?"

"It's not important. Look." I point to a door with an entrance panel that has an empty black circle in the centre. Placing my palm against it causes a small red light to appear. A second later, the elevator opens.

Hector laughs as we step in. "You aliens sure do seem to have a lot of the same tech."

I raise an eyebrow and press my hand to the panel inside the unit. The door closes and opens again almost immediately onto a different corridor.

"Not exactly the same." I step out.

"Not even a jolt," Hector murmurs.

"I guess you have to develop excellent stabilisation if you want to make an intergalactic colony ship."

Lights flicker on, revealing a thick red carpet. Someone wanted this floor to feel homey. We are definitely in the residential section. Now I need to remember where my family's quarters are.

I fell into a deep sleep for the last few hours on the shuttle. I dreamt about our new home with the blue sky and blue water. It was like standing on the beaches of Erot, but someone had altered all the colours. My skin prickled with fear and I began to run. Suddenly, I was being hunted by people who looked like me, only their skin was covered in mud and their hair fell in great knots around their shoulders. They carried knives and spears and chanted as they chased me along the sand. One of them slammed into my back and I screamed myself awake.

My mother took my hand. She too was fastened into her jumpseat. The whole shuttle was vibrating.

"What's happening?" I asked, terrified.

"We're docking with *Ofurion's* port." Mum smiled.

I began to feel nauseous again. I must have turned a funny colour, because Mum began to smooth circles around my palm.

"Don't worry, Nova," she added. "Once we're on *Ofurion*, things won't be so bumpy."

I took a big breath and tried to hold it for as long as I could. It's not what they told me to do in training. They told me to breathe evenly, but I found holding my breath much more effective at keeping my stomach contents inside my body.

Suddenly, the vibrating stopped. A loud thunk echoed through the ship, then Dad's voice came over the comms: "This is Fleet Admiral Starling speaking. All passengers be advised that we have now docked with *Ofurion's* port. Please prepare your unit to disembark. You may make your way to your designated disembarkation tunnel when the light in your cabin turns red. Once you've accessed the port, please go immediately to your onboard point." He paused. "I'll save my tedious speech for later. See you on the other side, folks!"

I heard laughter from the rooms next to ours. Mum unplugged her belt and then mine, before unloading our bags from the storage space in the wall. She placed one of the enormous bags onto the table and told me to check I had herded my dinosaur back into his safe place. I spent some time tucking him away amongst my clothes. Dad appeared just as I was sealing the bag. He checked I'd done it properly, then patted me on the back. "Well done, Nova."

"Thanks, Dad."

"Nova, it's time to start calling me by my title."

"Fleet Ad-mi-ral?" I spoke carefully.

"Exactly right. If we're in public, you must call me that, understand?"

"Yes."

"Yes, what?"

"Yes, Fleet Admiral."

Dad smiled and picked me up. He balanced me on one hip, then took a bag from the table. Mum shouldered the other. "Time to go, that light's been red for long enough," she said.

We marched along the corridor, then stepped onto a sliding floor. It sped us through a bare white tunnel. I'd hoped to see the stars, but no such luck. The port designers apparently found windows obsolete.

My parents stopped in front of a signpost. Dad clicked the letter M and we followed a set of arrows that lit up along the wall. We didn't see anyone else the whole way there and the onboard point was empty too.

"Where is everyone, Saros?" Mum asked.

"I arranged a private release so that we could get to our cabin without anyone seeing us."

"Is the threat that high?"

My father's lips pursed. "Ground Leader thinks the satellite wasn't an accident. We decided not to take any chances."

"How is Ursa?"

Dad let out a low laugh. "As bitter as ever."

Mum tutted. "How she ever expected to get the Admiral position with her vitamin D absorption rates, I'll never know."

"Her mind was always stronger than her bone structure. She'd probably have killed me herself, if she didn't know that I was the logical choice."

"Kill you?" I whispered.

Dad planted me on the floor and placed his hand against the onboard door control. "Nothing to fear, Nova. Your Fleet Admiral is invincible."

The door slid open and he walked through without picking me up again. Mum gestured for me to follow. We shuffled down another short tunnel and into the *Ofurion*. The floor was crimson. It looked like my bedroom floor. I tried not to think about who would live in our house now and whether they would change it all, strip away my home.

"Massnova, Meteora, Moon, Mooncycle ..." Dad read off the list of names. "Moonlight! Here we are."

"When can we be Starlings again?" I asked.

"We never stop being Starlings, Nova," Dad stated firmly. "Starlings are strong, smart survivors. It's in my blood, your mother's blood and your blood. But sometimes, in order to survive, we have to pretend to be Moonlight for a little while."

"Then when can I stop pretending?"

"When we reach the new planet."

I nodded; that seemed perfectly acceptable. I'd be in stasis for most of the journey anyway.

Hector and I walk along the corridor. Each door is marked with a family name, but there are hundreds of units on this floor alone. Still, we have to be close; the elevator should have taken me to the right floor based on my prints. Or so Marcus said.

"Have you remembered your name from before?" Hector asks.

"Yes." I cough.

"What is it?"

My mouth twists. I don't want to tell him. I've always been Lucky. Why should that change now?

"I, uh, I don't really know what I'm looking for at the moment." He runs a finger over the name 'Lunaress'. "I assume these are family names?"

"Oh, yes. You're looking for Starling." I pause. "No, wait. Actually, you're looking for Moonlight. My father kind of hid us."

"Okay ..." Hector gives me a sideways glance. "Want to talk about that?"

"Not really. I don't really understand why. Just that there was some threat."

Hector nods thoughtfully and begins to slide his finger along the right wall, observing every name with great focus. Suddenly, it occurs to me that Hector should not be able to read whatever language is written on the walls, but then I realise it's a longhand version of the language Infinity uses for programming. I sigh. *Marcus.* No wonder I've always been gifted with computers.

I ponder for a moment how Marcus and I picked up the native Infinitian language so quickly. Most of those who survived the Moon's arrival spoke the same language, and those who didn't learnt as fast as they could. As a child, I'd have been expected to pick the language up relatively quickly, but I didn't even hiccup. When my Infinitian family found me, I understood them from day one. And Marcus, he was an adult when he arrived. He should have struggled to communicate, but doesn't seem to have had any issues blending in.

As I run my thumb over the names on the left hand wall, I notice variations in the spellings of certain sounds. The Moon likely contains people who spoke a variety of languages from Urion. Perhaps we're all simply excellent linguists.

Hector's radio squawks into life. Belle's voice is just about audible. "Hello? Hector? Lucky? Can you hear me?"

Hector replies, "Yes. What is it?"

"Oh, thank the Stars! Is Lucky with you?"

I take the radio from Hector's outstretched hand.

"Yes," I say into the microphone.

"Look, Marcus called me. He explained everything. I'm so sorry. I shouldn't have – "

"It's fine." I cut her short.

She coughs. "I'm going to come join you, okay? Can you wait for me?"

"No. You need to stay where you are."

I hear her growl. It's not a noise I associated with Belle, deep and guttural. "I don't want to have this conversation over comms, Lucky. I need you to stop what you're doing and wait for me."

"I can't wait, Belle. It'll take you forever to get here from the caravan."

She curses under her breath. "Then I guess I'll just have to say it. I don't think you should try to release your father. In fact, I don't think you should try to release anyone."

"What?!" I snap.

Hector glances up from the name plaque he's deciphering.

"Something's wrong here, Luck. When I spoke to Marcus, the way he spoke ... I believe him about the whole alien thing, but my instincts are telling me he's not giving us the full story."

I press my forehead against the wall. "So what exactly do you suggest I do? Let everyone on Infinity die? Or are you asking me to murder everyone aboard this ship?"

Belle goes silent. I think she's put the comm down because I can't even hear her breathing. Then she says, "I'm asking you to think this through, to piece together what's actually happening before you do something stupid."

I snort. "Stupid? You think trying to save everyone is stupid?"

"No, that's not what I'm saying."

"No, no. Of course not. You think trying to save *my people* is stupid. Thanks for the vote of confidence, friend." I throw the comm back to Hector and continue working my way down the corridor.

"Lucky!" Belle yells.

Hector murmurs to her. I don't catch what he says. He looks at me, then says louder, "Don't come yet. Go to the cargo ship. Monitor the Moon and send warning to City if you see anything change, then drag the spare raft from the deck and get your arse here as fast as you can."

Belle says something back.

"Someone needs to do it, Belle. I'm sorry." Hector's eyes are watering.

My skin is still hot with anger, but I can feel guilt burning the pit of my stomach. Belle does need to stay behind; we need someone to warn City if things go wrong. And if she doesn't make it to Moon … Do I really want our last conversation to have been a fight? I shake myself. Nothing will go wrong, because she's wrong. *I'm doing the right thing.*

Hector slips the comm back into his pocket and returns to the door he was looking at. I watch him wipe his eyes across his scute-covered forearm and read the door label two more times before he asks, "Lucky? Is this it?"

I walk back to his side and stare at the name next to

his thumb.

"That's the one." I hover my hand over the silver panel. I don't want to think about the variety of potential scenes that lay behind the door, but I do.

Hector's hand slips into mine. He squeezes it.

"Whatever happens." He coughs. "I'm here, space-girl."

"Space-woman." I shove him with my shoulder plate.

Hector smiles and rubs his arm. He knows I'm teasing and would smile back if I could. He lets go of my hand and I press it against the panel. The door jams and Hector and I have to force it open together. The room is dark, except for a flickering light coming from the corner. As I move into the room, I see that it's one of the stasis pods. There are two. Mine, of course, is missing, launched as the Moon landed. My parents, however, were not. My father's pod is upright. It's the one that's flickering. Every flash of light reveals his face, exactly as I remember it. My mother's pod, however, is on its side. The ends are wedged between the wall and Dad's pod. There is no light inside. I don't want to look any closer. I'm fairly certain I know what I'd find.

Hector walks over to my father. He pulls a torch out of his pocket and runs it over the pod.

"This is ... something else," he whispers. He spots the engraving at the bottom and reads, "Say-rows?"

"Sa-ross," I correct.

"Well. It's good to meet you, Fleet Admiral Saros." Hector pats the side of my father's pod.

We're both now avoiding looking at my mother.

Hector clears his throat. "How do you open these things?"

I crack my neck. "Usually, they'd jettison and open automatically once the Moon finishes terraforming, but Marcus said to try the manual release at the bottom."

Hector hums. "It's worth a shot, right?"

I heave out a long breath. "Yup."

I place the sledgehammer and machete to one side and kneel down in front of my father's ... no, the admiral's pod and reach for the torch. Beneath the admiral's feet there's a red bar. I hook my fingers around it and pull as hard as I can. I think I hear a faint hiss. We wait a few seconds, but nothing happens. I pull it again. Again, nothing happens. I sit cross-legged on the floor. The path forward is now exceptionally narrow. Hector crouches down next to me and tries the pull bar for himself. He tries pulling it when the light is off and when the light it on. He even tries to time it somewhere in between. Nothing works, but Hector keeps trying until finally I say, "Stop."

He slumps next to me. There's a very long moment of silence. I'm looking at the man in the pod, trying to think of anything to say. I notice that we share the same double spiked horn on the knuckle of our forefingers. I think we sort of have the same nose as well, but it's hard to tell with the light flickering. He's biologically mine, but he doesn't feel real. He feels like a painting, or a story that I've told myself.

He probably would have been an excellent father in his own way. I guess I'll never know.

Stiff, I drag myself up off the floor and pick up the hammer. The glass of the pod is reinforced, so I summon all my strength to swing. I put my weight into my back leg, raise my elbows, tense my biceps.

Then his eyes flutter open. I drop the hammer. Saros' eyes gain focus on my face.

"Lyra?" He frowns in confusion and places one hand against the glass. The pod hisses loudly, the cover slips aside and he falls forward into my arms.

My father swooped down and wrapped his enormous arms around me. He swept me up from my chair at the dining table and span both of us around and around as he walked into the living area. I laughed and marvelled at how graceful he was. Even with all the twirling, he didn't knock a single item of furniture. It was like he had the floor plan of our little Urion home perfectly memorised.

He placed me down in his favourite seat and handed me my strategy sphere to play with. I smiled as he walked back into the dining room to talk with Mum and Uncle Doc.

Uncle Doc came once a month for a meal and a chat. He and Mum were in the same education group right up until specialism selection, but even after that they'd made a point of staying in touch. Mum always said it was important to know what the most regular health concerns were, so that you could build resistance or resilience into the next generation. Doc just called her his amicus. She made him laugh.

I sat fiddling with the sphere for a while, trying not to get to frustrated. Dad had set it to the highest level, so my success rate was only about 5%. But the best way to learn fast was to learn hard, or so my father said.

My ears pricked when heard Dad mention the *Ofurion*. At first I tried not to listen, but then his voice lowered and I knew he didn't want me to hear. "It almost overloaded today. Would have caused quite a bang." He laughed quietly. My spine tingled and my arms went all pimply.

"What happened?" Doc asked. I looked up to see my father scratching his chin uncomfortably. Mum was staring into her cup. Doc's face was hidden behind the dining room door. "I'm meant to climb aboard this thing in a couple of weeks, Saros."

Dad sighed. "It wasn't the ship. It was sabotage. But they caught the gashole and threw him out an airlock the moment they got the energy levels back to normal."

I started to shake. My thumbs had stopped working properly, so I sat clutching the sphere tightly in my hands.

"Sabotage?" Doc breathed. "That's the second attempt, isn't it? What if there's another?"

"We'll deal with it."

I stood up and threw my sphere down. The shell crunched against the hard floor. Mum and Dad looked up in surprise and I heard Uncle Doc shift in his chair.

"Nova, did you – " my mother began.

"I'm not going!" I roared. "I am not going!"

I recall we'd been having the same argument for months, but my rationale had been that of a traditional seven-year-old: I didn't want to go. My parents had easily logic-ed me into submission every time the topic came up. This time, though, this time my argument was 'I don't want to explode'. And I was not going to let it go.

My father's face darkened. "You are going, Nova." He stood and walked around the table to loom over me.

"No, I'm not! You can't make me!" I shouted.

His chest expanded and contracted very slowly. He crouched down. "Nova, there is nothing to worry about. The man who – "

"I am not going," I repeated.

He closed his eyes. "So you'll stay here then, all alone?"

"But I – "

He opened his eyes and stared straight into mine. "Nova, you can scream and shout all you like, but your mother and I are going. If you don't come, then you'll be here alone. That is your position." My eyes were watering. I didn't want to blink first. "I suggest you go to your room and think on that."

I held my position for a beat, determined not to look like I was following orders, then walked stiffly to my bedroom. Once my door had closed, I picked up an empty storage box and threw it against the wall. I needed to make one last defiant noise.

After that I burrowed into my bedding. Urion always ran cold at night, so I had plenty of layers to hide in. I hoped I could dig far enough into them that no-one would ever find me. They'd panic then. They'd have to search for me to find out if I was coming or not, but they wouldn't be able to find me and they'd miss the shuttle and get stuck on Urion. Where it was safe. Urion had certainly never almost exploded on anyone.

There was a gentle tap of scutes on my door. "Nova, it's Doc. Can I come in?"

I huffed. "Okay."

I heard my door slide open and shut. Uncle Doc let out a soft tickle of laughter. "You comfortable in there?"

"Yes."

I felt the weight of his hand press down on my shoulder. "Even if your mum and dad don't always seem to do what's right, they love you. You know that, don't you?"

I popped my head out the top of the blankets. "No. I don't."

I still don't remember his face, but I can picture the fluffy, purple brow he raised. "You don't?"

"No. No matter how many times they explain, I don't know why we have to leave. It doesn't make sense. Why can't they be happy here, with me?"

Doc smiled sadly. "Unfortunately, not everyone thinks like you and me, Nova. But they're trying to do their best for you."

"It doesn't feel like it."

Doc offered me his hand, and I let him squeeze the ends of my fingers. "I promise, though, if you get on the *Ofurion*, everything will work out."

"How? What if it explodes properly?"

"It won't. I know someone who's coming with us, and he's going to make sure everyone's safe."

"You do?"

"Yes." Doc started walking his fingers carefully across the tips of my knuckles. "I don't really want to leave either, Nova. However, my friend is going to make sure we get the best possible outcome from this trip. I'll introduce you when we reach our new home."

"I'm scared," I murmured, half into the blankets.

Doc pressed his chin to the top of my head. "I know, kid. But we'll be brave and go together. Alright?"

I mulled this over for a moment. "Okay." I sniffed. "But if we're making a deal, Dad says you've got to shake on it."

"The official deal-making handshake? Quite right, come on." Doc leaned back and I wriggled myself vertical in the blankets. He put his hand out, palm flat, fingers pointed toward the ceiling and spread wide. I placed my fingers carefully between his, each tip between the spikes of his knuckles. He gingerly did the same, although my hands were so much smaller than his that he had to bend his fingers awkwardly over my scutes. He smiled at me. "Right. Deal?"

I nodded and we shook our carefully knotted hands left and right.

I just about manage not to topple backwards under the weight of my biological father's semi-conscious body. Hector immediately jumps to his feet to help me guide Saros down to the floor.

"I don't understand," Dad mutters, and takes a lock of my hair in his hands. "Why is your hair red?" Then he touches my skin. "And you're so dark."

I take his hand in mine. I've never really been the kind of person who could comfort others with ease and now I'm struggling to find the words to tell him. I glance over at the fallen stasis pod.

"I'm, uh, I'm not Lyra, sir."

He tilts his head to follow my gaze. His chest rises and falls with a shudder.

"What happened?" he asks.

"Something went wrong during landing and, uh, only a few stasis pods jettisoned from the *Ofurion*. My pod went and, I don't know, I guess hers shook loose and fell over without mine there to support it."

Saros' head snaps back to me quickly. He pulls himself upright and studies my face. My eyes water and I look away.

"Nova, look at me," he says.

I close my eyes tight, lift my chin and open them again. He reaches out and touches my face. His hand is rough and calloused. *Like mine*, I think and smile.

"The starlight here has grown you well." Saros smiles back at me. "How have you survived for so long while we slept?"

"It's a long story …"

Hector coughs and Saros flinches, noticing him for

the first time. He fixes Hector with a familiar steely gaze. "Who's this?"

"This is Hector. He's an Infinitian, one of the natives of this planet. He helped me find you and get you out. I work with him."

"Lucky? Is everything alright?" Hector asks.

"Yes?" It's then I feel the change in my mouth as my tongue switches gears. I've been talking to Saros in our Urion language without even thinking. "Sorry. I think maybe my species have a weird knack for language." I turn back to Saros. "Do you know why I switch languages so easily?"

"Part genetic, part enhancement given at birth. I need him to speak more. Phonetic alphabet would be a good start," Dad replies.

I pass on this instruction to Hector and we run through the Infinitian alphabet and have a brief conversation describing how Infinity used to be arranged, and how it is now. Finally, Saros nods.

"I think that's enough – " he says in slow Infinitian. "Hello, Hector."

Hector's jaw drops, as does mine.

"I'm sorry it took … a while, but my brain is getting on and my time in – " Dad points at a pod.

"Stasis," I help.

"My time in stasis has muddled my mind a fair bit. But it is good to meet you. Can I expect all Infinitians to be uncoloured, fully scaled bipeds?"

Hector's jaw snaps closed, and suddenly he looks a little offended. "I'm sorry, what?"

"Your complexion, is that normal for Infinitians?"

"Um … well, normal for those remaining, yes. There are a few who look pretty similar to you, actually, but their families were from the Edgelands and most were wiped out when you landed."

"My sympathies for your loss." Saros begins to stand. I place a hand on his chest to stop him from falling forward. "Tell me, Nova, who else is awake?"

"Just Marcus."

"Marcus? That's not an Urion name."

Hector and I exchange a look.

"We could radio Belle and get her to contact him on my cabin's long-com," I suggest. "She could ask for his Urion name."

"No need." Saros stretches, bringing himself to his full height. He is a good foot taller than both myself and Hector.

Built for intimidation.

I bat the thought away.

"If we can get to the control room," Saros continues, "I can get the long-comms here working and we can contact anyone on Infinity."

My Infinitian parents once had their own children. They didn't talk about them, but there was a photo tucked in my dad's wallet. Once I asked who the two dark-haired boys were. Dad was silent; Mum told me they were my brothers. I asked where they were. She said they were with the Stars. Dad snorted.

It wasn't until I was older that I realised they'd died in the wake of the Moon's arrival. I felt guilty the moment I twigged, but I couldn't place why. I put it down to the fact that I'd asked questions about them in such a naïve way. Not that I could have possibly known any better at that age. Still, it hurt that I'd hurt my adoptive parents by bringing it up.

The realisation came alongside the decision to continue my training in City. I hadn't told either of my adoptive parents that I was planning on going back to the Moon. I knew just how weird it would sound. No-one in the Marshlands even mentioned the Moon. They only talked about "before": "Do you remember the cakes we ate before?", "I worked as a painter before – ", "Before, everyone had their own comms device." And in the middle of everyone else's nostalgia, there I was yearning to return to the thing that caused the after. So I kept my desire to myself until the last minute.

The day the solarflyer came to collect me for the science programme, we all cried. My mother died a year later from a virus with no treatment. My adoptive father still lives in the same little house in the Marshlands. At seventy, he's one of the oldest living Infinitians. We still write. He still signs his letters, "I love you".

What will he sign when he finds out my people killed his children from the before? Even if it was an accident.

Hector lets out a gasp as we enter the main control room. I guess it is kind of breathtaking, now the controls are all lit up.

"Don't touch anything," I say.

He holds his hands up above his head. "I wouldn't dare."

Saros smiles approvingly. "You have him well trained," he jokes in Urion.

"He's my friend. I don't need to train him."

That makes my father laugh. Then he notices the countdown display in the centre and points to it.

"What's this?" he asks in Infinitian.

"That's the time left until the *Ofurion* terraforms the planet and destroys everything."

He blinks. "Terraform?"

"Terraform," I state in Urion.

Saros frowns, clearly concerned by how little time he has to release everyone; only thirteen hours remain. As he starts reading off the panels, checking on the ship's status, I juggle words in my head: Saros, Father, Dad, Fleet Admiral. I'm at a loss as to what to call him, so I keep calling him everything. I think of the man who raised me, sat five days away in my Marshland home. My head is spinning. I want to sink to the floor again and feel the cool of the black surface against my skin, but something about the fleet admiral makes me stand up straighter than I ever have before.

Hector puts a hand on my shoulder. "You alright?"

"People keep asking me that question today."

"That's because today it's an important question to ask." He squeezes my arm and looks at Saros, who is now frowning at a blur of the *Ofurion's* data.

"I'm alright," I whisper. "I'm too busy to be anything else."

My father growls in Urion, "This makes no sense."

"What makes no sense?"

He sighs, switching to Infinitian again so Hector can understand. "I can't figure out why the pods didn't release upon landing. There's nothing in *Ofurion's* log to indicate what caused the problem."

"You should try and get hold of Marcus. He's the one who explained everything to me," I suggest.

"What does this Marcus specialise in exactly?"

"I don't know what he was on Urion …"

"He's been an excellent asset when it's come to advancing anything mechanical or computer based, Fleet Admiral," Hector offers. "When he finished his position as one of the first moon-sitters they made him a councilman in City."

"Moon-sitter? No! Never mind, I think I understand from context. So, this Marcus is a duo engineer …" Saros clicks his tongue. "We had plenty of polymaths on board *Ofurion*, but I wonder …"

"You wonder what?" I ask, but the fleet admiral is already fiddling with something on one of the consoles. He traces a pattern across it, then snaps up and walks across to the pillar with the glass orb. When he places his hand down, the whole ship hums into life. Hector's comm crackles and a trace of Belle's voice skips through, but we can't make out the words. The Moon's energy must be interfering with the signal. Hector looks at me, concerned. Belle probably picked up the energy spike in the cabin. She'll be panicking and so will the rest of Infinity when she sends the emergency warning. I shrug. If we can talk to Marcus, he'll keep everyone calm.

To Saros' left, a red light map of Infinity emerges.

"Where would Marcus be?" he asks.

I point to the brighter light of City at the centre of the continent and the map zooms in on my finger's position. Then I point at Civic Spire. It goes right to Marcus' office. I can even see the bright light of life sat in his chair.

"Is there a communication device in that room?" my father asks.

"Yes."

"I think I can pick up a general communication frequency in the building. Is that what would spark that device?"

"Uh, yes."

Saros rolls his fingers over the orb and the comm on Marcus' desk glows active. The life sign visibly jumps. Then Marcus' voice echoes around the control room.

"Hello?"

"Am I speaking to Marcus?" Saros asks in perfect Infinitian.

"Yes, this is he."

"May I ask what your Urion name is?"

"Oh, Saros! How lovely to hear your voice again,

amicus!" Marcus chirps in Urion.

"Aerglo Celeste, how did I guess? It would be you."

"Well now, that's not very friendly of you, Fleet Admiral."

"I would be friendlier, Aerglo, but I've just gone through the ship logs and the only reason I can see for the plan going wrong is that someone must have told it to go wrong."

"You mean the plan to quietly terraform a planet and colonise it? Yes, I don't know what went wrong."

Saros' brow lowers. He switches to a language I've never heard before. Hector taps me on the arm, noticing the difference. I shake my head. I can pick out the odd word, but not enough yet to figure out what they're clearly arguing about.

They begin to throw the word "stagnation" back and forth like it is the only word in the universe that matters to either of them. Finally, my brain clicks as Saros snaps, "Listen, you idiot, I didn't come here to make friends with the Infinitians. I came here to end the Stagnation, and end it I will. As soon as I figure out what you've done to this ship, I will release every Urion on board and send them to grind your bones to stardust."

Urion's capital city was called Marura. It was named for an ancient queen who, amongst other things, was a collector, curator and patron to many of Urion's most famous museums – the biggest of which sat (or perhaps still sits) in the heart of the capital. From what I remember, the building was ridiculous. Standard Urion architecture featured clean, simple lines. No flourishes. The only form of self-aggrandisement designers were allowed was to see how tall they could make a structure without it being a public hazard. Height was efficient, decoration wasn't. Marura's star museum, however, had been the tallest building in the city for centuries and was formed entirely from cast metal blocks. Under instruction from the queen, passed down through generations, the structure had been allowed to oxidise and flourish externally, but the entrance and internal spaces were regularly sanded and painted to avoid any such mutation.

As a child, visiting at the age of seven, I took in this information in silent awe. I'd never seen anything like it. My world was black and white and red, but here was a building covered with blues, greens and purples. The tour guide described in detail how the queen had chosen each metal from the local star system to remind Urions how their home stretched far beyond the ground beneath their feet. I wiggled my toes at that. Saros placed a hand on my shoulder. "Something wrong, Nova?"

"I like this ground."

His red brows furrowed in concern. "You know we have to go, Nova."

"But why?"

Saros picked me up and walked me away from the tour group. He ducked inside the front door of the museum and steered us into the exhibition on great Urion minds.

"Who's that?" He pointed to the portrait of a pale red-headed man with a large amount of facial hair.

I laughed. I didn't even need to look at the sign. "Great, great, great, great, great, great – "

"His name, Nova."

"Anatolius Starling."

"And what did he do?"

"He conquered our genome."

"Which allows us to?"

"Make people how they should be."

"Now, what's wrong with that?"

I frowned and let out a sigh. "We're the best at everything now, so now everyone's sad."

"Exactly. We know everything there is to know about the world around us, and our Urion spirit is dying of boredom. So we need to find a new lease of life. A new challenge." Saros nodded along to his own trail of thought. "Who's that?"

He pointed to another red-headed man, one that wasn't particularly familiar to me at the time. Now, thinking back, he looked strikingly like Marcus. I walked over to the plaque and read the name carefully: "Infinitas Celeste."

"What did he do?"

I frowned. My father knew the answer, but he always liked to stretch my linguistic processor. He cared more about building my vocabulary and understanding than the headaches it gave me. I continued reading with a pout. "He designed the first viable long-distance colony ship, including the faster-than-light-speed drive required for travel."

"And?"

I squinted. "While Celeste's invention was of considerable merit, it was undoubtedly an ill-advised project. Celeste believed that the way to create a perfect civilisation was through use of such ships to explore and expand across the universe, while the Urion government ruled in favour of the genetic sculpting programme created by Anatolius Starling. Despite this, Celeste privately recruited 10,000 souls and left Urion for the planet designated Q108_S7_P4, which is believed to be a habitable body with a singular land mass. To this day, it is unknown if any of the colonists survived." I shook my head a little; I felt like my skull was burning.

My father grunted. "They've not updated that yet. I'll have to have a word before we leave. We now know that Infinitas and his colonists survived. Our latest long distance scans of their planet suggest a thriving population, larger than our own, but inferior in quality. Traitors."

"That's where we're going?" I asked.

Saros nodded.

"I still don't get why."

Saros clicked his tongue thoughtfully. "They wanted to leave. They defied everything they were told. Their ideas and beliefs about what is right and wrong ... they're so different to ours, Nova. We'll reclaim their DNA, add it to our gene pool, and it will end the Stagnation."

I let out a gasp. Marcus clearly hears me and twitters happily in Urion, "Hey, Lucky! Did your translator finally finish the job?" My hands go icy cold and my heart races as Saros wheels around, jaw clenched with fury. "He's a real bloodthirsty bastard, your dad, did you know? Commander/War Class breed, 5th of his kind. Took them five goes to get the blend right. We're good at genetic sculpting, but predisposition is a bit of a fiddle."

"Shut up, traitor!" Saros snaps.

"Bah, I'm not a traitor! You're the gasholes trying to dissect my cousins because you, what? Got a bit bored? Aren't happy with the status quo?" I hear tapping on the other end of the line. Marcus typing something in at his desk. "You and your Stagnation can, frankly, plummet into the Void!"

The room suddenly plunges into darkness. I feel a hand grab mine and I try to pull myself free, but then my hand is planted firmly onto a head and I realise the person's too short to be Saros. Hector pulls at my arm and drags me toward the edge of the room. At the sound of our feet moving, Saros speaks. "Nova, stop."

For a moment, my body stiffens, like he's flipped some kind of kill-switch, but Hector is still towing me onward and fortunately he's strong enough to keep me going.

"Nova, I don't know what you're about to do, but

remember; there are 35,000 lives on board this vessel. I promise you, now I'm awake, they are not defenceless." It's a cold threat and it cuts me. I don't understand any of this.

Hector swings me into the corridor and I hear the door hiss shut. The light in the ceiling flickers into life. I feel myself falling toward the floor, but Hector grabs me and pulls me back onto my feet.

"Oh no you don't, soldier," he says shakily. "I think we need to get upstairs and grab those handy weapons we brought along. From the tone of that conversation, and how pale you've gone, I'm guessing we can't leave him in there alone with a bunch of buttons to push."

"There's no power."

"And I am putting that in the good-things-that-have-happened-to-us-today pile, yes, but I'm also guessing they didn't give your bio-dad admiralty over the Moon because he's terrible in a crisis. Come on." Hector nudges me along, towards an elevator. "Are you going to tell me what's going on?"

I call the elevator and we step inside. I open my mouth to speak when Marcus' disembodied voice fills the tiny room. "Hello there, friends!"

"You lying piece of – "

"I know, I know," he interrupts me. "I'm a terrible excuse for an Infinitian, but as Urions go, I'm pretty damn excellent, Lucky. I needed you to see what we are."

"And what's that, exactly? Maniacal, genocidal freaks from outer-space?"

Marcus coughs. "I mean, yes? Pretty much. Was that

not clear?"

I slip down the wall and bury my head between my knees. I feel dizzy.

The Moon killed everyone on purpose.

"Hi, Councilman Marcus. Hector here. Could you maybe fill me in? Lucky's, uh, indisposed for further conversation right now."

"She on the floor?"

"Yes."

"Understandable. Right, well, long story short, all you folks calling yourselves Infinitians actually come from a planet called Urion. Now your Urion brothers and sisters have come to add you to their genetic sculpting programme, because they think it will make them more interesting and stop them from feeling like they've peaked."

"That, uh, doesn't sound so bad."

"They deliberately caused cataclysmic natural disasters as a method of population control upon arrival, and they don't intend on sampling your DNA the fun way, if you catch my meaning."

"Cosmos be kind." Hector looks down at me. "Okay, I also understand why Lucky's on the floor now."

"What I don't get is why you lied to me?" I talk into my knees. "Why couldn't you tell me what the Moon really was, instead of spinning me some lie about it terraforming the planet? Void, why couldn't you tell me who *I* really was?"

Marcus sighs. "Here's the thing ... if I'd told you that 35,000 Urions, including your biological mother and father, got on a ship with the intention of destroying another civilisation, would you have believed me?"

"Yes."

"Lucky, I lived with you for ten years, and I only ever saw you look at the Moon with awe on your face. You knew what destruction it caused, but still a little bit of you thought, *that thing's beautiful!'*

"So what? So what if I didn't believe you?"

"So then you would have got your beloved Saros out of stasis, trying furiously not to believe me. You would have helped him get everyone else out of stasis too, and that would be it. Endgame. Infinity's culture sucked up into Urion blood via needle, and they'd still feel just as pleased and bored with themselves. Gasholes."

"You realise that you're an Urion, right?"

"Exactly. There's the irony. The Urion race think they're somehow going to fix themselves by absorbing the ideas of Infinitas Celeste and his colony through their descendants' DNA, but they already have those ideas! Stars, they kept my bloodline so pure I might as well be Infinitas. But they've never once listened to a single member of my family, Lucky."

"So you did all this to get their attention?"

"Not only that. I also wanted to see what would happen if I gave you the scenario; Infinity or the Moon?"

"And?"

"You did exactly what I hoped you'd do. You found a way around it."

I punch the wall of the elevator so hard that my scutes leave a dent. Then I pull myself up off the ground. "And what now? What exactly is your endgame?"

"I want you to do what I could never do; I want you to convince a true Starling to do things the Celeste way."

I felt like I was suffocating. Then I opened my eyes and realised that I actually was suffocating. I was inside my stasis pod. Through the glass I could see grey plumes of smoke and a blue sky. The yellow sun dazzled me. I gasped for breath and threw my arms forward against the pod cover. It was programmed to respond to any sign of distress with release, so long as the atmosphere was breathable. To the relief of my seven-year-old self, my pod began to hiss as it flooded with Infinity's air. Finally, the glass slipped back and I stumbled out, expecting to land in the arms of my mother or father. Instead, I got a mouthful of red moss and cut both my hands on black rock. I let out a yelp, and then sat there in silence. If Saros found me crying over a few cuts he'd be angry, so I balled my fingers into tight little fists to stem the bleeding and looked around.

I knew in my gut that something wasn't right. Mum had told me that when the pods landed, they would land in clusters in safe regions of Infinity's landscape, but there was no-one nearby. The only sign of life was a grey stream of smoke coming from deep in the jungle.

"Hello!" I yelled, but no-one responded.

I waited for as long as I could, but no-one came, so I got to my feet and plodded into the thick of green and red. The canopy was so dense that I struggled to keep track of the smoke. Fortunately, the smell of fuel and fire was strong and then the sound of someone crying drifted toward me.

"Hello?" I called again. Still no-one responded and the crying continued.

Eventually, the thick emerald light gave way to a stark spotlight of yellow. It was a freshly cut clearing, containing two stasis pods. One sat neatly upright in the dirt, empty. The other had landed glass-first on a sharp black rock, similar to the one I'd cut my hands on. The resident of the damaged pod was not moving. The Urion from the upright pod was clinging to him and weeping uncontrollably. I'd never really seen an adult Urion cry like that before. My maternal grandfather passed away about a year before we left our homeworld, but not a single tear was shed. Saros said that tears were for the dying, not the dead.

"Are you hurt?" I asked the crying Urion.

He screwed his face up at the sight of me and cried harder. "Why is this happening?"

"Are you dying?"

He let his long red hair fall over his face. "She's only here because you couldn't bear to think of her frozen forever. She's only here because you couldn't bear to think I might kill her."

"Are you talking about me?"

He lifted his head and looked me straight in the eye. "Nova Starling. I want you to know that because of you, the love of my life died today."

I swallowed hard, not really understanding. "I'm sorry."

His face cracked and tears came rushing from him eyes again. He wept and wept until exhaustion kicked in. Unsure of what to do, I took off my over-layer and spread it across his shoulders. He looked at the tiny item of clothing clinging to him and said somewhat sarcastically, "Aren't you sweet?"

"Thank you," I answered, because it felt polite.

I looked up at the body of the Urion in the crashed pod and recognised the face of Uncle Doc, every single inch of it. His lips were blue, his expression calm. He hadn't woken before he died.

Thank the Stars.

I felt my face scrunch up. The red-haired Urion took the thick band of titanium from Doc's wrist and slipped it over his left hand. It clinked against the matching band he wore. Saros and Lyra wore similar ones made of platinum. The Urion then curled up on the floor next to Doc's pod.

"Sleep. That's what I need. Maybe this nightmare will be over when I wake."

I sat down on the floor in front of him and stared at his closed eyes.

"What is it, Nova?"

"Who are you?"

He grunted. "The biggest joke in this universe." He popped open one eye. "Aerglo."

"Oh. Where are my parents?"

"They're stuck in stasis."

"How did I kill Uncle Doc?"

Aerglo frowned at me. "Doc made me change the plan for you and I didn't have time to run the proper calculations, so he died."

"Oh." I stared at the lifeless form hanging out of the pod and I felt something terrible rumble through my body. My eyes grew wet. My throat tightened. Suddenly, I let out a wail like I'd been stabbed.

"Shit!" Aerglo said, probably because he'd never seen an Urion child above the age of two let rip in such a manner. "Shit, shit!"

He scrambled upright, span me so that I no longer faced the pod, and pressed me hard against his chest. "Stars, forgive me! I didn't understand, Doc. She is different. Shh, kiddo, shh. I'm sorry. I'm so sorry."

Hector has the machete slung over his shoulder, but he's dragging the sledgehammer along the floor. It makes a high-pitched squeal against the polished metal.

"Can't you carry that thing properly?" I ask.

"It's heavier than it looks."

I take it off him and lean it against my shoulder. It's heavy, sure, but it's nothing to complain about.

"If you're meant to be negotiating, are you sure it's a good idea for you to have that?"

"What do you mean?"

"Won't you come off as a little threatening?"

I let out a small laugh. "I don't think Saros is that

easily intimidated, but you can have it back before we get in there, if you like?"

Hector frowns.

"What?" I sigh.

"Just noticing that you didn't call him 'Dad' or whatever."

I shrug. "If everyone on this ship were awake, if I'd grown up with him and my bio-mother, I'd be calling him 'Sir' or 'Fleet Admiral'. He'd have me strung up for calling him anything else, I'm sure."

"Are you? Sure, I mean?"

I blink at Hector.

"What?"

"Are you sure that what Marcus is saying is entirely true? That your whole species really decided to massacre most of mine, so they could … I guess experiment on the rest of us?"

I look at the floor. A wave of shame floods my stomach and I feel nauseous. "I only remember bits and pieces of Urion, Hector, but what Marcus says tallies." I take a deep breath and grab his wrist. "I'm sorry for what we did."

Hector laughs in surprise. "Lucky, you don't have to apologise. You didn't plan this. You didn't make this happen."

"No," I say, letting him go. "But I feel like at least one Infinitian should hear it from an Urion."

He rests a hand between my shoulder blades. "I think you're far more Infinitian than Urion, Luck."

I hum in response. I'm not so sure. After all, I wasn't just content to sit and watch the Moon. I had to be the one to crack it open and see what was inside. I made this mess to solve my own Stagnation. Urions seem to be particularly adept at causing chaos. Then I think about Marcus and Doc. Marcus is a troublemaker for sure, but he's done nothing but help rebuild Infinity since his arrival. And Doc, all he ever did was look after the sick and injured.

So maybe it's being a Starling.

"Hey, can you two hear me?" Marcus' voice spat out of Hector's com.

"Yeah. How are you – "

"I'm using the Urion tech in my quarters. It cuts through the interference. Lucky, have you made a decision?"

I huff. "Marcus …"

"Look, I know you don't trust me, I know I've lied to you, but surely by now you remember – "

"Marcus, shut up!"

He snorts. "Why am I not surprised? You Starlings are – "

"Don't you dare say we're all the same." I feel something inside click into place, like I've been struggling to right myself for the last few hours and I've finally managed it. "You know full well I am *nothing* like them."

"So you remember that, huh?"

"Yes. And I remember that you have a nasty habit of saying shit you don't mean when you're stressed, so hold your tongue, Aerglo. I'm not going to do things the Starling or the Celeste way. I'm going to do things the Lucky way."

"What's that mean exactly?"

"We'll find out shortly."

Marcus sighs. "Well, I've set up the door to respond to your prints. It'll open when you're ready to do whatever it is you're going to do."

"Good," I reply. "Now, radio silence."

Hector switches his comm off to make sure no-one else can get through. We don't want anyone interrupting while I try to talk my father down from total genocide. When we reach the control room I hand the sledgehammer back to Hector and he tries to balance it the same way I had. "I'm genuinely beginning to think you might actually be stronger than me. We need to arm wrestle when this is over."

I chuckle. "You're on."

I turn to the door and plant my hand on the silver panel. When the doors part, they reveal that Saros has already managed to get the lights back on. As we enter, he is lying underneath a sleek, black console, staring into a box of crystals and wires. However, the moment he notices us, he slides out and onto his feet in one smooth motion. Seeing the sledgehammer and machete, Saros charges at Hector, but I step swiftly between them and plant my palm in my father's chest. It's not an attack, as such, but it winds him. A move that he himself taught me before sending me to my first Urion children's social event. They were somewhat, uh, energetic experiences.

Saros rubs his chest. A smile crawls onto his face and a quiet laugh escapes his mouth. "Glad to see you've not forgotten everything I taught you, Nova."

"You'll have to forgive me. It's only been a few hours since I've remembered I'm not Infinitian. Some things return faster than others."

His eyes widen a little at that. "How is it that you came to forget?"

"I had a near-death experience. A group of Infinitians found me and raised me as their own."

"So Aerglo didn't raise you?"

"No," I state. "But he was my mentor."

Saros sighs. "Nova, are you with me, or him?"

I shake my head. "You're making an incorrect assumption."

Saros smirks and takes a step back. "And what's that?"

"That you're on different sides to begin with."

"That man killed your mother."

"By accident," I say firmly. "He also killed Uncle Doc."

"Stars ..." Saros mutters.

"You both want to end the Stagnation for the Urion. He killed two people by accident. You've purposefully killed, how many?"

"Approximately six billion," Hector states.

The number hits me like a lead pipe. It's not news. It's something we were taught in school, but it's the first time I've attached that number to the man in front of me. I look at Saros and he sees the outrage on my face. Something flickers behind his eyes.

"Nova, they were Infinitians, not Urions."

I let out a cackle. "Are you kidding me? Okay, you want to absorb new ideas and end Stagnation? Let's start by getting this one through that extra thick skull of yours, Father: all life – regardless of how developed, intelligent or carefully genetically crafted it might be – is *life*, so if you purposefully take it away you are committing *murder*. If you do that on the scale you have, that's *genocide*!"

Saros shakes his head. "What ideas has Celeste filled your mind with?"

I raise a hand. "No. No. This is not Marcus talking. This is me. Nova. Remember that little girl who couldn't understand why we had to come here in the first place? The child that you spent hours trying to rationalise this whole expedition to? That was me, and I'm telling you now, as a grown adult who knows the whole truth, that the Stars will not forgive this atrocity. Not if you continue down this path. And neither will I."

Saros puffs his chest. "And how exactly do you propose to end the Stagnation without absorbing the DNA of the Infinitians?"

I smile. "Not everything is about DNA."

"You want us to talk to them then, as Celeste suggests? Do you realise how little change that will bring? How little movement for this generation and the next?"

I tilt my head. "You can still be in motion, even when you're sitting still."

"Explain."

"I've sat on this planet for thirty years, staring at this stupid sphere, trying to figure out why in all the Constellations I spend every night dreaming about it.

But I've also grown in ways you couldn't have possibly predicted, because you think every Urion is born already perfect. You think your Stagnation is a sign you've run out of momentum because of your genes. I think it's a sign you've stopped paying attention to what's around you. Go look at Infinity with your eyes, take it in. Let Urions figure out how to survive on a planet with a yellow star and a bright blue sky. Then, yes, get to know the locals."

I look from Saros to Hector. Hector's face is pensive. I know why. I didn't expect Saros to dust away the killing of billions of Infinitians so breezily either.

"And what about the Infinitians?" he says sternly. "Do you really think they will want to talk to the people who destroyed six billion of their kind?"

Hector grunts.

"Your friend doesn't seem to think so?"

"No, I think we'd be willing to talk if you were," Hector corrects. "I was laughing because you clearly know we're sentient enough to be pissed about that sort of thing."

Saros sighs. "We always knew you were sentient. Our peoples have only been separated for a couple of millennia. But you betrayed us, took precious DNA across the universe and frittered it away meaninglessly."

"And ... what did Marcus call it? 'Genetic sculpting' worked so well for you? Made you all so happy that you lived in paradise and didn't feel like maybe you'd programmed restlessness and dissatisfaction into your bones? Yeah? Great." Hector puts the sledgehammer and machete on top of the console behind him and rolls his shoulders until they click. "Our civilisation may not have been perfect before the Moon arrived, but at least we didn't go slaughtering the neighbours every time we felt a bit bored."

My father's red brows furrow. There are a lot of new thoughts rumbling around in his head and none of them lead to pleasant conclusions. If he accepts any of our ideas, it means redefining his own mission as criminal. And that's putting it mildly. He might not ever face punishment, but he will have to live with the weight of what he's done. And he will have to convince 35,000 Urions to live with that same weight. His eyes are fixed on the console beside him. A small smile creeps around the corners of his mouth.

As I make this silent notation, Belle bursts through the open door, wielding the upgraded hunting pistol Marcus left in my care. The gun had been stored under my clothes, the pellets in the back of my computer's casing. From the way Belle sweeps the barrel left and right, I know it's loaded and instinctively lower myself. Then she aims the barrel at Saros.

"We have to go, Aerglo," I said, tugging on his arm.

He sat in the dirt, staring at Doc. Infinity's insect population had already moved in. The previous night I'd watched Aerglo fight off a couple of mid-weight scavengers, but he couldn't repel the tiniest predators.

"Aerglo, I'm hungry," I moaned.

He didn't flinch.

It wasn't the first time I'd tried the hunger tactic. I'd been hungry for days, picking at nearby bushes and praying that their fruits wouldn't kill me. My skin had started to turn dark shortly after I'd eaten my first mouthful, and I genuinely believed I was dying. Now I realise it must have been the yellow sun altering the pigment in my skin, as my parents had described on the shuttle.

Staring at Aerglo, my eyes began to water again and my face grew wet. The tears fell silently. I lay down on the ground and let out a small sigh.

For some reason, that made Aerglo look at me. He peered over curiously.

"Are you really real?" he asked.

I frowned. "Yes."

He gradually got to his feet. Astonished, I remained perfectly still on the floor. I was afraid that if I got up he'd sit back down again. He walked over to me and stared down.

"You're crying again, kiddo."

"I'm sorry."

"No. No. It's alright. It's rather refreshing, actually."

"Like rain?"

Aerglo laughed to himself. "Yes, just like rain. Come on." He offered me his hand and pulled me up from the floor. He breathed in slowly, then, without looking at the broken stasis pod, hissed the words, "Bye, Tide."

I glanced over my shoulder and whispered, "Bye, Uncle Doc."

Aerglo squeezed my hand, then we started walking back the way I'd come, out of the jungle terrain.

"Have you noticed all the colours?" I asked.

Aerglo raised a brow. "What do you mean?"

"There's a lot more colours here, aren't there? Look." I waved my hand at the greens and reds of the foliage around us.

"We had these colours on Urion. The sun was red. Your hair is red. Your science textbooks would have been green, or at least they were in my day."

"Yes. But there's *more* of them here. Urion was all black and white and red."

Aerglo thought for a moment. He stopped when we reached a large tree wrapped in hundreds of tiny blue flowers and smiled softly. "Okay, Nova. I concede. There are more colours here."

I nodded proudly. "The sky is blue like those."

"Is it?"

"You didn't see in the clearing?"

Aerglo shook his head. "I didn't notice."

"That's okay," I said happily. "We'll see it again soon."

I skipped ahead through the undergrowth and brought him back some berries, which I recognised as ones that hadn't made me ill. We each had a handful and continued our trek out of the jungle.

"Stars, you've made this planet bright!" Aerglo exclaimed as we reached the edge of the tree line.

I ran towards my pod and then turned back and spread my arms wide. "Look, Aerglo."

He plodded to my side and turned, taking in the

immense variation of tones splattered across the landscape. My eyes started to leak again. I was still sad and scared, but I did like the colours a lot.

"My …" Aerglo breathed.

"We should count them," I demanded.

"I thought you were hungry."

"I am, but we should count them."

He looked down at my wet face and tutted, but not in the way Saros or Lyra tutted. Aerglo crouched and pulled his sleeve around his hand to gently dab at my cheeks. "We will count all the colours we know, and name all the ones we don't as we go. How about that?"

I nodded. "Okay."

"But you have to promise me something."

"What?"

"When we find people, you must only use their words for things, and never ever say you're from another planet."

"Why?"

"I will explain when you're older, but you have to promise me this. Otherwise I won't be able to protect you, like Uncle Doc wanted me to."

"Are you going to help Mum and Dad?"

Aerglo sighed and placed both hands on my shoulders. "I will give them a chance. I promise."

"Then, okay. I promise too."

Instinctively, I shove myself between Belle and Saros,

blocking her shot. My father peers over my shoulder at the hunting pistol. Belle twitches the barrel. "Get out of the way, Lucky."

"I can't do that, Belle. You don't understand what you're doing."

She shakes her head. "No, you don't understand what he's doing." She aims the gun at the spot between Saros' curious eyes. I put my hand in front of his face.

"I know exactly what he's done, Belle. We're trying to convince him to stop doing anything else."

"He's already doing it!"

"What?" I glance over my shoulder.

Saros takes a step back from me and raises his hands. "I don't know what she's talking about, Nova," he says in Urion.

I turn back to Belle. "What do you think he's doing?"

"The ocean around the Moon has been heating up exponentially."

"Well, the Moon is active now. It's bound to get a bit warmer."

"When I left the cargo ship it was forty degrees and still increasing. I could barely stand to put my feet in it by the time I got the spare raft in the water. It's not normal heat radiation."

I spin on my heel. "Explain."

Saros has backed all the way to the orb console. I see him debate his next move. He snaps a crystal out of the hole in the console he'd been working on. In an instant, I see how sharp the freshly broken edge is and notice his whole body shift toward Belle. I look him in the eye and he realises I know what he's about to try. A proud smile flutters across his face, but he doesn't stop. He lunges his enormous form at Belle, faster than she can react. I react for her. I step to the side, half crouch and thrust the dense armour on my elbow up into my father's gut. He tumbles over me, dropping the crystal. We both scramble for it, but I reach it first. I swing around to face the threat, and in doing so, impale Saros in the side. He scrambles backward onto the floor. Belle lines up her shot again, but I smack the gun out of her hands.

"What the Void?!"

"I'm not done!" I roar. I kick the weapon across the room. Hector takes Belle's hand, as he took mine earlier, and drags her away from me. His eyes are wide, and he won't look at me. I try not to notice.

I loom over my father. "What exactly was the plan here, Saros?" He grimaces, trying to shuffle himself toward the orb. I place my foot lightly over his hand. "Answer me."

"Dark Star!" he curses. "Fine! I set the engines up for a launch. I was going to give the planet another quick bump. Thin the herd a little more."

"And you weren't going to mention this?"

Saros laughs. "Why would I do that? You'd only try to make me stop."

"Were you even listening to me and Hector?"

Through all the pain he must be in, he smiles at me. "I got the gist."

"You were playing for time."

"You caught me."

I close my eyes, shifting weight into the foot on Saros' hand. He doesn't make a sound. Neither do I, but I want to scream.

When I open my eyes he is grinning all over his face.

"What?" I say darkly.

"I'm glad to see some of the Starling spirit in you." I stare at him, so he continues, "This is the way we do things. If you want something to change, you don't talk about it, you fight for it."

"Are you trying to make me kill you?"

He tilts his head, still beaming. "That's the only way you're going to get control of this ship." He wriggles his fingers beneath my foot. His scutes are stuck in the thick sole of my footguard. "It's the only way the Urions on board this ship will ever respect you. After all, if you kill something, you're clearly its better." He looks at Hector and Belle. Belle tries to charge at him, but Hector is keeping a firm grip on her arm.

I grit my teeth. "You were never going to listen."

Saros snorts as he turns back to me. "The Infinitians aren't worth *knowing*, Nova. Their only value is in their DNA."

I pull my foot off his hand and begin to walk slowly across the room. The admiral chuckles. "Even these two, look at them shivering over there. Such cowardice. On Urion we'd have destroyed their stock before it had a chance to spread. We'll definitely have to strip that predisposition out. Your mother would have loved that puzzle, my girl."

I reach the console where Hector dropped our

weapons. My hand wraps around the handle of the sledgehammer. As I pick it up it feels lighter than before, entirely controllable. I turn.

"I'm telling you, Nova, you're a Starling. Give the people on board *Ofurion* six months on this planet and you'll see, what we have planned will be endlessly better than what these mutts could ever achieve." He doesn't hear me approach over his own drivel. "You could provide excellent insight too, I'm sure. With your knowledge, we'll make short work of selecting the best traits to keep from the Infinitian line."

Belle and Hector gasp as I raise the hammer above my head. Saros looks up just in time to acknowledge that he's about to die.

"Oh," he says, before I crush his skull.

"What colour is that, Nova?" Aerglo asked me.

I swallowed hard and it felt like my oesophagus was cracking. My whole mouth was bone dry. I hadn't had anything to drink all day and there was nothing to block the sun on the old mountain road. My skin had grown darker and darker. Aerglo, however, had gone incredibly pink, even purple in some spots. Moving seemed to be causing him a great deal of discomfort.

"Nova? Come on, what colour is that flower?"

I sat down in the dirt and sighed. I tried to summon some saliva. When none came, I flopped backward and whispered, "Sitter-red."

Aerglo crouched down next to me. "We need to keep going, kid. You can't stop here."

"Thirsty," I managed.

"I know. Hopefully we'll find a river soon. You know they start up on top of the mountains? So this foot trail probably runs over one, or near one, eventually."

I closed my eyes. "Tired."

Aerglo took my hand in his. "Me too, Nova. Come on."

I shook my head back and forth, slowly. I couldn't summon the energy to shake it vigorously. The ground felt oddly comfortable. I wanted to sink into it like a mattress and never get up again.

Aerglo grabbed my shoulder and shook me. I snapped my eyes open and scowled at him. He laughed, but something about his expression seemed more concerned than mischievous. He put his hands under my armpits and hoisted me onto my feet. I swayed, he steadied me.

"We have to keep going. You can't stop like that again until I say, okay?"

I wanted to cry, to show him how exhausted I was, but no tears came. He took my hand and pulled me forward.

We walked and walked and walked. The yellow sun began to fall behind the mountain we'd spent the morning walking around. Still, there was no river and no sign of life. I noticed Aerglo's skin beginning to flake. The scutes on his elbows were shedding, leaving behind raw, unprotected skin. He dropped my hand to check himself. His joints were clearly tender, but he tried to hide how much it hurt.

He looked at me, then off down the trail. I watched as he ran through various plans inside his head, and debated the outcomes. He sighed, took my hand again, and carried on walking. This time he moved with urgency. His stride was extended, so I practically had to run to keep up. My feet failed almost immediately and I tripped over myself. I sprawled face first into the dust and grit, unable to raise my arms to brace my fall.

Aerglo cursed under his breath and then said, "Nova, I'm sorry. Please, get up."

I wanted to; I flexed my fingers, felt Infinity crush up under my nails, but I couldn't put enough energy into my arms.

"Nova?" Aerglo placed a hand on my shoulder, but he didn't shake me this time. "You can't move, hey?"

I wriggled my fingers again. He placed his hands over mine, "Okay. I'll just have to carry you, then."

He carefully turned me over, then hooked an arm under my knees and shoulders. I heard him hiss as the grit scraped at his skin. I tried to protest, to move myself again, but I couldn't. He lifted me and my weight against his arms made him growl. "Why wasn't I built like your father? He'd have managed this no problem."

He took one unsteady step. I felt his body waver, then he rushed forward, sprinting with me in his arms. I stared at him, feeling the breeze of motion across my face. His facial expression ricocheted back and forth between fierce determination and immense fear, until, in the last wisp of light, I saw exhaustion hit him. He stumbled, but in his fall made sure to twist so that I wouldn't be harmed. As his back met with the ground he let out an animal roar of pain. I didn't move. I stayed in his arms until he found the energy to sit up and perch me next to him. He looked at me.

"I'm sorry, Nova."

I squeezed one of his fingers numbly.

"We can't keep going like this."

I blinked.

"I can't, I can't …" His face scrunched, but he also couldn't cry.

He lay me down on the ground and rolled me onto my front. I heard him stand and take a couple of paces. Then he came back.

"I want you to know, kid, I'm only doing this because it's what's best."

Then everything went black.

As I swing the sledgehammer down for the third time, I hear a scuffle behind me.

"Belle, don't!" Hector pleads.

I turn and see the barrel of my gun being aimed at my head. Belle holds it with both hands, jaw stiff, eyes tight. I drop the hammer.

"What are you doing, Belle?" Hector asks.

"Didn't you see what she just did?"

"Yes, I did. But she – "

"She didn't have to use a sledgehammer!"

"Look at me, Belle. Isabelle, please." Hector says slowly.

Belle's eyes stray from my chest to his face, but I stay perfectly still. Shock is crawling up my spine, freezing me in place.

"I know that was brutal. I was scared too, but it's over now, Belle." Hector continues.

"But Lucky – " Belle looks at me and I close my eyes. I can't make eye contact right now.

"She saved us. She stopped an evil man from continuing to do evil things."

There's silence in my head where there should be thoughts of grief and guilt. I open my eyes again quickly, because I can't stand the nothingness. Belle's arms are beginning to bend, the tip of the pistol sinking toward the floor.

"I just, I – "

"Give me the gun, Belle. Everything's going to be alright."

Her body relaxes completely and Hector untangles her fingers carefully from the weapon. He tucks it into his waistband, then wraps his arms around Belle.

"Let's go out into the corridor, okay?"

Belle nods into his chest. Hector tentatively steers her out of the room. He gives me a look over his shoulder. He's not as calm as he's pretending to be. The expression on his face stinks of worry ... and fear. He doesn't know what I'll do next. Neither do I.

As their voices drift away down the corridor, I collapse onto the floor. I pull my knees up to my chest and tilt my head up to stare into the ceiling light until my eyes water. Then I close them, and resign myself to the darkness behind my eyelids. Loneliness sweeps through my body so fast I choke. I drop my forehead onto my knees. None of this is right; none of this is how I wanted it to be. And now I have a choice to make, and there's no-one to help me make it.

"Even if your mum and dad don't always seem to do what's right, they love you. You know that, don't you?"

Doc's voice rattles around my head. A sob escapes my chest.

They loved me ... and I –

I hear a single set of footsteps return.

"So that was the Lucky way of doing things. Not quite what I expected," Hector says. He's trying to sound jovial, but it's forced. His voice quivers on every note. "Lucky?"

I don't look up; I can't look up. I'm to busy trying not to think about the body a few feet away from me.

"Come on, Luck. We should go."

I sniff.

We should go. But there are things that need to be done first.

Steadily, I pull my head from my knees and blink to clear my eyes. I wipe my face with my arm.

"We need to, to turn the engine off," I stutter and pull myself to my feet.

"How do we do that?" Hector asks.

I stagger across the room and pick up the machete. Then I stumble back and kneel beside what used to be my father.

"Lucky, you – " Hector starts.

I make short work of detaching the hand from the corpse. I embrace the static thrumming inside my mind. I have to be fast. I can't be emotional.

"Stars ..." Hector whispers.

I bring the hand over to the orb and press it against the glass. I place one of my index fingers next to that of the still warm limb. Marcus told me that the Moon would need a conduit to a living mind to tell it what to do. I think about the engine and a holographic screen appears in front of me.

With my spare hand I scroll through the list of options and stats, until I find the button to tell the engine to shut down. The Moon shudders. I hadn't really noticed the vibration while it was happening, but now it's gone the room is filled with an extra cloud of silence and stillness. I stare into the red light projection.

If they loved me ...

I think about all the frozen lives aboard the Moon. I wonder how many of the Urions know love, how many would be willing to compromise their ideals to keep that love?

How many are like Doc and Marcus? And me.

Hector's hand touches my shoulder nervously. I blink, and like that the projected screen in front of me changes, listing the number of stasis pods aboard. There's a button to access the manifest and a button to release.

Hector's hand tightens. "Tell me you're not thinking about doing what I think you are?"

I open my mouth, but nothing comes out. I raise my hand and access the manifest. I scroll through the list of names; it's endless.

"Lucky, you're scaring me."

I close my eyes, try to summon some kind of comfort to my tongue. Instead what comes out is, "I can't let them all die in here."

"They're not going to die, Lucky. They're frozen."

"And what happens when the Moon runs out of energy? Marcus said there was a failsafe, but that was part of his lie. Urions are far too arrogant to install that kind of thing. They'll all just stay frozen until there's nothing left to revive them."

"They'll kill us, Lucky. You heard Saros. They'll pick every Infinitian apart for spare pieces."

"But what if – "

"What if what?"

"What if there's someone on here like Marcus, or like his orbital, my Uncle Doc. Doc was the kindest being I've ever met. He's the reason I'm here and he died because of it." My hand is clamped so tightly around Saros' that his double horned knuckle has split the skin of my palm. "They're not all bad people."

I feel the muzzle of my pistol press against the back of my head. "You can't do this, Lucky."

I stare into the red light of the screen. Over the roar of mental nothingness I decide Hector's bluffing; I decide if he's not bluffing, I don't care.

No-one else dies today.

I lift my chin and flick my spare hand at the screen. "Sorry, Hector."

The Moon begins to rumble, the whole room shakes. Hector's hand slips from my shoulder. The gun falls.

He was bluffing.

Belle rushes back into the room.

"What's happening?" she yells over the noise.

I turn slightly, still holding on to the orb and the hand. Hector can't take his eyes off me; they're glazed over with disbelief. "She's set them all free."

"What?!"

"She's released them all."

"Move!" Belle shunts me out of the way and grabs hold of the pedestal. She slides her hand over the glass, but the screen in front of her doesn't change. Anger sweeps through her body in a way I've never seen before. She turns to me and lashes her hand out across my face. Luckily, her scutes are hard, but not sharp, so she only leaves a bruise. Still, I'm knocked sideward and have to pick myself up off the floor. I leave the dead hand where it fell.

Hector is holding on to Belle again, but she's growling to be free like a rabid animal. I need to leave. As I walk past them, Belle spits at me and yells, "You're a murderer, Lucky! Do you hear me?!"

The words bounce off me into some dark void. I walk out of the central control room and begin to run. All around me the Moon is vibrating and the ceiling lights have shifted to a blue tone. I begin to feel sick to my stomach, but tell myself it's all the motion. I continue running. My legs don't ache, my breathing is steady and my heart rate even. Maybe I'm not

Infinitian or Urion, maybe I'm an actual machine.

It doesn't take long to reach the Moon's entrance at a run, but the ship hums to me the whole way, getting louder and louder, filling in the crevices of my mind that the static hasn't found. I try not to think about Hector and Belle cowering at the Moon's heart. I try not to think about what they think of me. I open the Moon's door and rest myself on the edge.

A few seconds later, there is a triumphant boom that deafens me. I watch in awe as thousands of pods scrape across the sky, trailing fire and smoke. I try to count them, but they seem infinite.

As the first pods disappear over the horizon, the Moon lets out another blast. My stomach churns. Suddenly, I retch forward into the water. The remnants of my breakfast spill into the ocean. I wipe my mouth and curl up on my side in the doorway, watching the second swathe of pods rocket into the distance. I begin to feel how hot my body is. I'm burning alive.

The static in my mind is clearing. Thoughts begin to float to the surface.

I've betrayed my friends.

I've torn Infinity apart.

Stars, I killed my father today.

I press the heel of my hand into the core of my chest, where I'm sure my heart should be. I try to feel it beating, but between the vibration of the Moon and the thickness of my armour it's not possible.

My chest feels hollow.

The Moon blasts free a third wave of pods.

"Think before you speak, Lucky," Marcus said.

We had just finished giving a tour of the cargo ship to a group of councillors. I had rounded up with a speech on how, whatever the Moon was, it was obviously made by a far superior species.

"I don't get what your issue is. It clearly is made by some race that is way ahead of us tech-wise. Even before the landing, we had, what? A couple of rudimentary spacecraft and satellites? Nothing even close to – "

"That's not the point."

"Then, Stars, Marcus, explain it to me!"

Marcus wagged his finger at me. "That word, 'Stars', do you know where it comes from?"

I scowled. "No."

"Centuries ago, long before the Moon's arrival, our people worshipped the celestial bodies above. The Stars helped us grow crops, allowed us to see predators, kept us warm; so we prayed to them."

"What's that got to do with anything?"

"That worship died out here, and phrases like 'Stars' and 'Cosmos be kind' became old-fashioned and out-dated. That is, until the Moon landed. I saw it happen, Lucky. Overnight, those phrases went from forgotten fossils to as common as the Stars themselves. A *moon* had fallen out of the sky and killed billions of friends, family, loved ones. All people could do was start praying again, even if that's not necessarily what they thought they were doing."

My scowl turned into a frown. "I mean, that's interesting and all, but connect the dots for me here."

"Okay. Put it this way, do you want to start a war?" Marcus asked.

I raised a brow. "No?"

"Then do not tell people – people who were so terrified that they resurrected their long-dead gods – that the thing that wiped the majority of them off the surface of their planet was made by a 'far superior species'."

"Okay. I take your point." I perched on the desk as he ran through some numbers the chief councilwoman had asked for. "But it's not like whoever made that thing is ever coming back for it."

Marcus glanced at me sideward. "Never say never."

"What? Even now, you think aliens are gonna rock up to collect this thing?"

"Stranger things have happened, Lucky."

Acknowledgements

Firstly, a big thank you to all the members of The Writeryjig Clubamabob, who have read sections of this novella in various states of stupid. ALL of your input encouraged me to keep going and to keep filling in the blanks of this world.

Thank you to Rachael S and Amy for lending me your science brains, so that I could keep my beaches sandy and my tech techy. Additionally, Ian, you get a very special thanks for helping me toe the line between rampant aestheticism and the basic laws of physics. RIP, lighthouse; you are gone, but not forgotten.

Tori, Queen of Commas, thank you for bearing with me through this and for reading *Moon-Sitting* so many damn times. Thanks to Jo for helping me make the ending exactly what it needed to be. Rachel T, thanks for being WC's eternal powerhouse of literary enthusiasm, and for sending that energy my way when I was running low. Rachel E, thanks for taking the time to ease my paranoia and for telling me what *Moon-Sitting* is actually about after I'd rewritten it and rewritten it … and rewritten it.

Much gratitude to my family for letting me live rent-free while I practiced that special kind of madness called re-drafting. Dad, you get a prize for telling me to stick with this style. Mum, you get one for your artistic eye.

Finally, Kit, thanks for letting me pet your head when I was stressed and living in a blanket.

About The Author

EM Harding hails from Wales. She started writing seriously at the age of eight (she was a very serious child) and received her first rejection letter around the age of nine. She now holds a BA in English with Creative Writing and an MA in Applied Linguistics (both from the University of Birmingham). She runs a writing group known as "The Writeryjig Clubamabob" – a name that even she can't spell without looking it up – and is an active member of the Twitter #WritingCommunity.

She is also guardian to an illustrious chicken thief named Kit.

Moon-Sitting is EM's first novella and first foray into the world of self-publishing. It's been an adventure.

Twitter: @EM_Writing
Website: www.emmort.wordpress.com

Printed in Great Britain
by Amazon